OPERATION HYACINTH

THE STORY OF FORBIDDEN LOVE

Pawel Kurczab

For more information contact:
Riverdale Avenue Books/Magnus Lit
5676 Riverdale Avenue
Riverdale, NY 10471

www.riverdaleavebooks.com

Design by www.formatting4U.com
Cover by Scott Carpenter

Digital ISBN: 9781626015623

Trade Print ISBN: 9781626015609

Hardcover ISBN: 9781626015630

First Edition November 2020

Operation Hyacinth (Polish: Akcja "Hiacynt") was a secret mass operation of the Polish communist police, carried out in the years 1985–87. Its purpose was to create a national database of all Polish homosexuals and people who were in touch with them, and it resulted in the registration of around 11,000 people.

Officially, Polish propaganda stated that the reasons for the launch of the action were as follows:

- fear of the newly discovered HIV virus, as homosexuals were regarded as a group at high risk
- control of homosexual criminal gangs
- fighting prostitution

However, most probably, the Służba Bezpieczeństwa (SB) functionaries wanted to gather compromising evidence, which would later be used to blackmail involved individuals. Furthermore, those persons would be more willing to cooperate with the security services.

Operation Hyacinth, upon order of the Minister of Internal Affairs Czeslaw Kiszczak, began on November 15, 1985. On that morning, in different colleges, factories and offices across Poland, functionaries of the SB arrested numerous persons suspected of being homosexual or of having connections with homosexual groups. Those arrested had special files entitled Karta Homoseksualisty (card of a homosexual) and some of them were talked into signing a statement:

I (first name and last name) have been a homosexual since birth. I have had multiple partners in my life, all of them were adult. I am not interested in minors.

Apart from signing the document, those arrested were ordered to give their fingerprints, some of them were blackmailed into describing intimate parts of their sexual lives, and some were blackmailed into denouncing their colleagues.

The operation lasted until 1987, but files were added until 1988. It has been estimated that some 11,000 homosexuals were documented, and these files are now called "Różowe kartoteki" (Pink card index).

Due to Operation Hyacinth, members of the gay community decided to go "underground" and cover their sexual orientation even deeper, several of them left Poland and the operation itself was criticized by Western mass media. The Polish government denied all allegations of such a program. Jerzy Urban, spokesman of the Polish government and overseer of Operation Hyacinth, when asked in December 1988 by Kay Winthers of *The Baltimore Sun*, said that such an operation never took place. (Wikipedia).

This novel takes place in 1985 in a city called Szczecin, Poland, during Operation Hyacinth.

For Tomek,
the Man of my Life.

Acknowledgements

I'd like to thank my editor, David T. Valentin, who worked tirelessly with me on many rewrites to develop this novel, originally written in Polish, to its current form.

14TH NOVEMBER 1985

As always, the alarm went off at a quarter to seven. Kamil stayed in bed for a while longer, but finally, indolently got up and out of his bed. The sun had already risen, casting its orange light over the city, but when Kamil peeped out of his flat's window, the blocks in his district were still grey, boring, concrete chunks, as if they were still asleep. The omnipresent dreariness was extremely depressing and just made it harder for Kamil to get out of bed.

Yet another dull day, he thought. *Thankfully it's Friday tomorrow and finally two days off work.* He turned on the radio. As always, channel three. *Jestem Kobietą (I Am Woman)* by Maanam was playing. He became lost in thought as he mindlessly prepared breakfast. He made two sandwiches with some paprykarz szczecinski (Polish canned fish with rice and spices), which he has loved ever since he was a child, and then he thoroughly brushed his teeth.

In the small kitchen with celadon walls, he always sat squeezed between the benchtop and the table that occupied most of the space. Faced towards the window as he ate, he watched the large chestnut tree growing in the yard and the birds on it. He spotted a red squirrel twice. Each time it was jumping from branch to branch.

1

Moving from the kitchen to the bathroom after dropping off his plate in the sink, he walked through a narrow corridor with light brown paneling on the walls. He tripped over a small red rug lying on the floor. The small, stuffy bathroom was always pedantically clean, with the white tiles on the wall, the sink and the small bathtub resembling an atomic shelter toilet rather than a standard middle working-class washroom. *Luckily, I don't need to shave because I hate doing it*, he thought. He always shaved in the evening, just to gain a few more moments in the morning. He threw a few splashes of water on his face, brushed his teeth, and headed out for the day, somewhat ready but not at all excited for the work day to come.

* * *

He passed a city prison on Kaszubska Street on his way to work. Because the cell's windows faced the street, one could always, even in the early morning, see a variety of women standing on the sidewalk trying to pass information to their husbands, fathers, sons and lovers despite the cell's windows being placed considerably high and there being a huge wall. Although strictly illegal, because of the restrictions on visits and the specific location of the building on the main street, none of the prison employees intervened and they turned a blind eye to these kinds of activities.

Some of the women shouted right from the street where they stood, and the men answered from the cell windows.

One of them, in her forties, was poorly dressed in a black mini skirt and a lemon-yellow tight sweater along with dirty old brown shoes with worn-out heels, which were most likely taken from church charity parcels sent from abroad. She had greasy short black hair and badly done, over-the-top makeup. Her Tarry black eyelashes from excess mascara and carmine lipstick made her look like a cheap whore from a nearby dive after drinking all night long.

She screamed, "Ania has had a baby yesterday. It's a boy. They will come by to see you next week. Darek got a B in Polish. We love you and we are waiting for you!"

Oh God, how sick is that? How can she make herself into such a whore? Do these people not have even an ounce of self-dignity? Fucking scumbags. On his way to work, he picked up some fresh buns for lunch from his favorite bakery, which, at this hour, wasn't yet so busy. More people were coming out to the streets and the cars; buses and trams moved swiftly, like a previously wound up mechanism in an antique watch. Kamil stepped over the same potholes in the pavements that had yet to be repaired after many years. The old pre-war, post-German tenements, built with gusto and grandeur in every detail, still remembered the Prussian Empire at its zenith. The times when Szczecin was a large port city put on a par with Hamburg, was forever now gone. After the war, the ports were taken over by the Polish communist government who would never allocate any funds for their restoration.

Old gray plaster was peeling off the walls leaving white unsightly patches resembling vitiligo patches on the skin. The old peeled paint on the front doors looked like a dry desert lake. Now, patches of plaster were dropping off them and they were in a need of some serious maintenance work. The faces of people Kamil passed in the street were sad and dreary. It was rather cool, and in the air, you could sense a slowly coming winter. Drowsy Szczecin was slowly waking up to life.

When he reached the building of WUSW, the Voivoship Office Of Internal Affairs, he saw the staff frantically running around the corridors from one room to another. He's now worked here for a few months right out of university thanks to his father's friend's connections, who was employed in one of the departments fighting with anti-state activities in the country. The building itself was a huge edifice in the old, post-German style. Before the war, it used to be where the Marine Authority Office was located, but afterwards the Office of The Housing of Recovered Territories was placed here, only for the whole WUSW to be moved here later. The building remembered the times of its great notability—massive, brown, oak doors with adorned handles leading to each of the rooms, high ceilings and corridors stretching forever. Kamil was never fully sure how many rooms there were in total in the whole building. Once he had heard there were about 210, other times about 170. There were eight Departments in the building. For each, there were four Divisions. Each of those had separate Sections, from A to F, which reported directly to the Provincial Office of the Interior (WUSW) in Szczecin.

The Divisions from the first floor carried out preliminary investigation activity, ones from the second floor administrative and legal activity and the third floor focused on operational and technical activity. Each Department employed between 80 and 100 people. All Departments cooperated closely with the MO, ZOMO and ORMO.

Officially, Kamil was employed as an official in the MO, but because of his personality, and because of the specific and occasionally dangerous nature of his work, his position was intended for much more difficult and demanding tasks and actions than those assigned to the average militia officer.

After presenting his badge, he finally reached Division B, where he had recently started to work. Entering the office, he bumped into his friend, Robert, who worked at a desk next to him. Robert was 35 years old, had green-grey eyes and wispy blond hair. He was married and had two children. Rarely did they talk about their private lives. They mostly talked about sports and cars. They worked together well because they were both attentive and meticulous when working on the files, and Robert was always happy to help because he had a lot more experience in the job.

Kamil spotted a pile of new folders, about 20 black thick folders that his department had asked him to check for just that day. The folders mainly contained intelligence from various militia informers and infiltrators, as well as their latest reports and deletions and anonymous tips. *Yet again this will be one of the most hard-working days of the month,* Kamil thought

"Hey, how's it going?" shouted Robert.

"Here again, as you can see," Kamil laughed.

"The boss wants to see you at 8:30 in his office," said Robert, fixing his shoe.

"Me? What for?" Whenever he heard the boss wanted to see him in his office, he felt alternately confused and somewhat nervous. In his mind, the fact that he had no wife and children was enough to make them want to transfer him to a unit in another town. It was a paranoia of his that he couldn't get over. He had grown fond of his place now and felt quite at ease there. He had never liked sudden changes in his life.

"I don't know. Something to do with our operation on those *others*. After all, you know what's coming on Friday."

* * *

The boss sat in his armchair with his back to the window, looking through daily press: *Trybuna Ludu* and *Głos Szczeciński.* He was around 60, severely over-weight and reeked of sweat. He always wore the same, grey, shabby blazer, which had the same stains from a year ago. There were two pink-red warts with gray hair growing out of them, one under the eye, and the other near his lips, which always disgusted Kamil. Additionally, when Robert spoke or explained anything, his boss would spit around. That was probably why he always reminded Kamil of Khrushchev.

"Oh, it's you Adamski," said the boss, putting his newspaper aside. "Sit down. We have your files here." The boss opened Kamil's file. "A skilled and intelligent graduate of sociology at the University of Szczecin, 5'10", brown hair, hazel eyes, likes sports, volleyball in particular. Practices three times a week in a sports hall with Stal Stocznia.

"Since the first year in High School you were a member of the ZSMP, a member of the Polish Socialist Youth Union where you were praised and given several awards for your activity. Employee of the Year in spreading socialist ideology and culture,

Medal of Dedication and Courage for sacrifice in numerous actions, Employee of the Year in promoting physical culture.

"A member of the party for over three years. Single, for now. You write very good op-ed pieces for our magazine about the increase of the standard of life of our citizens. *This* is the kind of people we need, and we take good care of." The boss paused for a moment and peered over Kamil's folder. "And how is your new flat?" he asked suddenly.

"Good, thank you. Even though I've only lived there for three months, I've settled in and arranged it to my taste." Kamil coughed up, surprised that Robert was even asking about Kamil's well being. "I am obliged to the Division for helping me allocate this quickly."

Kamil was angry with himself for having to grovel before the boss, but he knew that being allocated a studio apartment in three months' time was completely unattainable for an ordinary citizen. As a single bachelor, it was impossible to find an apartment in a new block close to the city center. Families with children had priority in allotment, and even then the real waiting time ranged from eight to 12 years. Housing construction was often delayed and dragged on for years due to the socialist economy and the constant shortage of basic building materials.

"As I said, we need people like you," the boss repeated, closely staring at Kamil. "Tomorrow, as you know, Adamski, we are launching Operation *Hyacinth*. As per the orders of the supreme, we will set up a folder for each and every faggot in this city. These are going to be hardworking days since we've counted that there are around 2,000 of these scum here." The boss grimaced at the thought. "We will ask about contacts, friendships, partners, work and details of their sex life. You have only been here for around six months, but we have, let's call it, a special task for you."

"What task would that be?" Kamil asked, completely baffled by the turn of events.

In his mind, Kamil vaguely knew what he might need to do. Once recruited into his division, Kamil was sent to participate in special training to test his memory, perceptiveness and logical thinking skills. The training had a duration of four weeks and covered both theory and fieldwork. In the field, the exercises included following a suspect, taking pictures while hiding, and arresting suspects in a very discreet way so as not to attract the attention of bystanders. Participants were also taught the art of camouflage and the pursuit of a suspect. He also had a knack for anything technical. Only after passing all tests and training was he qualified and assigned to the appropriate unit. With his unique set of skills, he was often tasked with missions of disguise and surveillance.

"From tomorrow on, your name is Andrzej Górecki. Style your hair differently and stop shaving for a few days just in case. Since you were so good at memory and observation tests and activities, tomorrow morning at the MO headquarters we want you to sit in the corridor among those called for questioning and memorize their faces, phone numbers, names and surnames, as well as listen to what they are talking about. They will most likely be scared, so they will start talking to one another. Besides, they more or less know each other, because it is a very well-sealed society. We must identify as many enemy elements in the Resistance who are threatening to destroy our socialist system. Remember that this includes each and every domestic enemy unit that overtly resists the communist authorities in Poland and the USSR.

"Such units can be dangerous to our system, and some of them keep in touch with foreigners, because they are mostly just male prostitutes. Apart from that, we need to limit and control this rabble, before AIDS begins to spread in our healthy, working national collective," the boss kept on chaffering, proud of himself. "Many of them will cooperate, because they're hiding their tendencies at home, work and schools. Do not talk too much, rather just listen. The interviews will last a few days. At the end of the day, you will write down everything you have memorized and pass it onto Markowski from Division B1. For now, that will be all. You may leave," he finished, glancing at his watch.

* * *

On his way back home, Kamil saw his neighbor stepping out of the staircase. He was completely blind and lived next door to him with his wife. They had had a baby a month ago. Even though he was blind, he would walk to the clinic every day, where he worked as a masseur. Kamil was so proud of both of them that, despite the difficulties, they were trying to live normally. *Would I ever be able to find such determination within myself?* he wondered for a moment. After all, he's always tried to take the easy way out.

Even after getting home, he still thought about his task. *Are the homosexuals as dangerous as the boss had said? Why do all this? We will look ridiculous asking them about sex.*

9

When it comes to homosexuals, Kamil didn't dislike them or anything. He didn't really care about them. He believed there was a rather small number of them since they were hardly seen in public. And besides, none of his friends were one. The only connotation he had with them were the movies *Czterdziestolatek* and *Wielka Majówka.*

Well, he thought, *a job like any other that just has to get done.* Anyway, he has been trained and prepared for much worse tasks during his business and training trips.

Before going to bed he turned on the radio for a while:

> *Ktoś znów wczoraj mówił mi:*
> *Trzeba przecież kochać coś, by żyć*
> *Mieć gdzieś jakiś własny ląd*
> *Choćby o te dziesięć godzin stąd*
> *Wciąż jestem obcy*
> *Zupełnie obcy tu—niby wróg...*

> *[Eng.*
> *Yesterday someone told me again:*
> *To feel alive you need to love something,*
> *You need your own piece of land,*
> *Even if it's ten hours away*
> *I'm always an outsider*
> *a complete outsider here, like an enemy.]*

Listening to Lady Pank (an all-male Polish rock band, very popular in Poland in the 1980s and is often dubbed the Polish Rolling Stones) Kamil began to fall asleep. So, he turned off the radio and went to bed.

15TH NOVEMBER 1985
Militia Headquarters, Mazurska Street in Szczecin

From the early morning, the headquarters was full of confusion. Precisely at 8:00 o'clock, the first people were brought in for the interviews. At around 8:20, Kamil casually left the bathroom unrecognized and sat down on a bench among those waiting. Every now and then, new Nysas van, transported more people in. The whole range of the society was there—starting with elderly men all the way to university students. Some wore uniforms typical for shipyard workers, others wore everyday clothes. There were also those who had perfectly tailored suits made to order, and two people with white doctor gowns. At half past eight, the first name was read out and the person was asked to enter room five. Surprise, shock, fear, shame, confusion and doubt twisted on people's faces. You could see that some of them knew each other as they exchanged meaningful looks.

Kamil did everything to act naturally. First, he took three deep breaths, making sure that nobody would notice. He put one hand in his pants pocket and started crushing the peppermint candies that he always carried with him because he had the impression that his bitten cheeks gave him bad breath. He put on a carefully studied, indifferent face and thought about an imaginary funeral for his mother. Whenever he saw it in his mind, he became artificially calm and silent, so much so that he didn't respond to any external stimuli. He tried to blend in with the crowd as much as possible, constantly reminding himself not to lick his lips. But despite his efforts his heart started quickly pounding. Finally, due to the stress, he gave in to biting the inside of his cheeks. He never bit his nails because he was disgusted by any germs festering under them.

Fuck! What am I doing here among all these weirdos?' he thought. *'Why the fuck was I chosen for this?* For a moment he thought that the whole task was beyond him. He had envisioned it to be much less complicated. He was surprised at his own panic, but he quickly remembered that he had been assigned this task because the boss trusted him. He also knew it was too important a job and he couldn't screw it up. If everything goes well, he would certainly get a promotion and a raise soon. That thought calmed him down.

He got up, walked to the window and asked a grizzly man in his fifties for a cigarette, despite never smoking prior. But he had to remain calm, blend in. He couldn't give away his cover. He had to act natural.

"Sure, why not?" said the grizzly man, turning his back to the window.

Kamil thanked him for the cigarette and slowly began to smoke it, making sure not to inhale. *Shit, I hope I don't choke. That would be a hell of an embarrassment, and what's worse, they might realize they're being set up.*

"What's this operation?" The grizzly man asked. "Why have they brought us here?"

"I don't know," Kamil said, trying to keep his calm. Even so, he couldn't control his rapid heartbeat or the sweat dripping from his brow. "I'm just waiting like all the rest."

"So how long have you been waiting?"

"Around half an hour." Kamil answered more quickly and nervously than he liked.

Suddenly, the door to one of the rooms opened and the first interviewee came out, a skinny man, well into his thirties, tall with his hair cut short. He had a drowsy face, as if he just heard something upsetting.

"What do they ask about?" asked a young boy. He was a dark-haired young man 20-some years old was wearing blue jeans and a burgundy corduroy jacket that looked imported. The white summer sneakers suggested that he had to dress in a rush, as autumn mornings were already crisp cold by November. He didn't look like a fag like the boss had described.

"Not here. I'm going to the loo," the other answered the skinny man.

Three people from the corridor followed the first interviewee to the toilet. Secretly, Kamil joined the group. When he was using the toilet, he heard, "It seems to be something big. They asked about work, friends, and if I have any connections to the resistance. They also asked if I have any colleagues abroad, and then, at the end, they forced me to write and sign some idiotic statement about my partners. Fuck, it's all sick!"

"Why go through all this?" someone from the group asked.

"I don't know, maybe they're looking for someone?" the interviewee answered.

Kamil did his best to return to the corridor in the

most slow and natural motion he could muster for someone who just wanted to zip out of a room full of infidels.

The information from the toilet spread quickly amongst others waiting in the corridor. All those previously speaking stopped, and a strange silence covered the place. A few minutes after 10:00, the last transport of the day came. Soon, the corridor filled with at least a hundred new people who all looked as equally anxious as the last batch.

How am I supposed to collect any information here? All I want to do is run from it all, he thought.

A few of the new people sat down on the bench next to Kamil. The last of them, a blond guy of average height and blue eyes, looked curiously straight at Kamil.

Shit, he probably knows me from somewhere. Kamil got frightened and started to pretend to be reading a newspaper. After a while of reading, he couldn't stop himself from looking back at the stranger again. Their eyes met and Kamil felt somehow weird. He has never felt like this before in his life. It was abashment, shyness and some odd excitement at the same time. He has been trained in case of various, and even odd, situations. And yet he was completely unprepared for this.

He stood up vigorously and came up to the window to see the stranger without having to look at him directly. He wore jeans, probably made by the Oder (the only company making jeans in this Communist country), brown trainers and a maroon shirt. He was holding a dark green, polyamide coat hung over his forearm. He had sharp, masculine facial features with a strong jawline, and a fit body. Kamil thought that he must be fancied by a lot of women. A few moments later, he realized that he has never looked at or paid attention to another man this way, as if looking him up and down and assessing his level of attraction like Kamil should've been doing for a woman. After a couple of deep breaths, Kamil took a walk towards the exit and back. He felt a thin layer of sweat on his palms as he nervously rubbed the tips of his fingers over them.

Kamil took a glimpse at his watch. It was almost 1:00 p.m. Suddenly, the door to room four opened.

"Next, Andrzej Górecki."

For the last time, Kamil took a look at the stranger as he began his stride to room number four. Their eyes met again, and the blond guy smiled.

The room was small and stuffy. Two standard desks and two chairs made it look as predictable as the next 20 rooms in that same building. The dark blue curtains were half-shut, which made the room dark. Two policemen were in the room. The senior officer was about 50 years old and grey-haired, sitting at the desk with a lamp on. The younger man was roughly 30 and blond-haired, sitting at the other desk and leafing through the morning newspaper.

"That's it for today. We are taking you off. You may go home," he heard from one of the two policemen sitting at the desk. For a while, his thoughts were still preoccupied with the incident at the corridor and he didn't fully understand what the official had said to him.

"Oh, yeah. I understand," Kamil coughed up.

"Besides, we are finishing up with these faggots anyway," added the older, grey-haired policeman.

The second policeman was clearly amused. "Oh, use the back door of the station to leave, so that no one can see you."

22ND NOVEMBER 1985

Militia Headquarters, Mazurska Street in Szczecin
Interviewer—captain Cegielski
Scribe—second lieutenant Tokarczuk
Interviewee—Zbigniew Fabisiak

Two desks and four chairs were placed in the inter-rogation room. Old, yellow curtains almost didn't let any daylight in. The floor, which was covered in ordinary, grey PVC sheets, made the whole place seem even gloomier than it already was. There was a black lamp and a telephone on each of the desks.

Cegielski was drinking his coffee and smoking a cigarette. The young second lieutenant Tokarczuk was noting everything down on an old typewriter. He looked just like a clone of the senior captain.

They had the same uniforms and the same blasé faces devoid of feelings. Fabisiak thought as he entered the room.

HOMOSEXUAL'S CARD

"Name and surname?"

"Zbigniew Fabisiak."

"Parents' names."

"Adam and Maria."

"Age?"

"Forty-seven years old."

"Address?"

"Santocka Street 16/2, 71-083 Szczecin."

"Profession?"

"Actor."

"Place of work?"

"Teatr Współczesny in Szczecin."

"For how long?"

"Since 1976."

"Close family, wife, children?"

"Don't have any. I'm single."

"Come on, Fabisiak. That's bullshit! You're 47 years old and you're single! You better admit that you prefer men!" shouted Cegielski.

The policeman jotting down notes laughed quietly.

"My life is my private business," Fabisiak tried to backchat. Fabisiak tried to act confident. He sat up straight with his chin up and maintained eye contact with the policeman when answering questions. But that didn't stop him from sweating and he felt that his voice was about to break down if the interrogation was to continue as aggressively as it was already going. He was afraid his eye would start twitching any minute and he would melt down completely.

"Well, well! Don't even try to fuck with me!" the interviewer screamed. "We, too, know a lot about you. The whole theatre was buzzing about your affair with Komornicki, before he ran away to Berlin. Not to mention you bugging youngsters in the Kasprowicz Park. Oh... your mummy would not be happy knowing the kind of pervert you've become! After all, she is all you have left, and her health is not so good. Such information could kill her. Besides," Cegielski carried on with a sadistic satisfaction, "the manager of the theatre, Paprocki, also wouldn't want to keep such a deviant in his troupe. You know, it would be hard to get into a different theatre at this age," he paused. "In fact, it's a rather small society."

"What kind of men do you like?" Cegielski asked after a while in a humorous voice. "Although, looking at you, it probably doesn't matter."

The policeman taking notes at the other desk laughed out loud. He had a morbid expression and looked like his education had stopped at primary school. The policeman noting at the second desk snorted with laughter.

"And in bed, do you play the role of the woman or the man?" he kept on mocking him.

Fabisiak did not answer any of the questions, but tears filled his eyes. He had never felt so degraded and humiliated as he did now. He could feel the last fraction of his personality being taken away. As if someone had spat straight into his face.

"And what roles have you taken lately?"

Fabisiak was still silent.

"Oi! Answer me when I speak, or this *will* end horribly for you." The chief looked Fabisiak in the eye from so up-close that Fabisiak could clearly see his tired bloodshot eyes and unfortunately took a whiff of his bad breath. There was spit on his lips that looked like foam. The chief stared at Fabisiak with so much hatred that his facial expression resembled that of a hungry, ravenous dog who had just chased down his prey and was about to tear it to death.

Cegielski threatened with an expression of a winner.

"A butler in *Śluby Panieńskie* and Dyndalski in *Zemsta,*" Fabisiak answered, half crying. These were *two 19th century Polish plays written by Aleksander Fredo.*

"These don't seem to be leads, but some supporting roles. Have you never been a lead in any play?" Cegielski asked mockingly, knowing very well the answer to his own question already.

"Not yet. But everybody says I'm the best in supporting and background roles."

Fabisiak felt he had just been dealt a major blow, as painful as it was paralyzing. For years he had been cast only in supporting roles, which made him angry, bitter and frustrated all at once. He knew he was better than many of the actors at his theater. The problem was, he'd never carried that much clout and couldn't bring himself to be as shameless in fighting for parts. His innate lack of self-confidence, coupled with his quiet and soft personality, meant that he was never be taken seriously and was mainly cast in secondary roles. He also refused to suck up to directors. Perhaps those very traits reflected his private life as well. Being gay, he'd never managed to be in a stable relationship with someone, even though he used to be very handsome. Sooner or later, all his partners would leave. Casual sex in parks or public restrooms only aggravated the feeling of emptiness in his life. All he had was his work at the theater, and he couldn't imagine doing anything else at his age.

"Well, well, 47 years old and not even one lead role, there must be something wrong with you, then?"

The second policeman laughed ironically, again.

"And when was the last time you saw Komornicki?"

"I can't remember. It was a long time ago, before he left for Berlin."

"Did he not send any letters?"

"No."

"Any messages passed by your common friends?"

"No. Nothing."

"That's hard to believe, because he has been seen in Szczecin two months ago. We know he had connections to the enemy of our state. Soiled tissue paper was found in his house after he fled to Berlin. People like him must be exterminated," Cegielski hissed through his teeth. "Remember, you tend to go around different groups and you know various people. If you do happen to hear anything important, you have to report it to me right away. Or else...Well *you* know what. That's it for today." The expression on his face melted from pleasure and mockery to boredom, as if all of this were just a game to him. Then, he pointed to the statement with a dirty finger and said, "Sign the statement and you are free to go."

The younger policeman passed a pen and a sheet of paper with the statement already written on it to Fabisiak.

I hereby declare that I, Zygmunt Fabisiak, am a homosexual since birth. I have had numerous partners during my lifetime, all of age. I am not interested in minors.

"Why do I have to sign this?" exclaimed Fabisiak.

"What? Do you want me to lock you up for pedophilia? Is that what you want? If your cell mates found out you're a wiener, and if you started to wave your handbag around, you would not last two days there."

Both policemen burst out laughing.

Fabisiak signed the document. When signing the document, he didn't care. Again he felt like trash. He was afraid to think about what would have happened if he hadn't signed the paper. Should his mother find out he was caught having sex with younger men in the park several times, she would have a heart attack right away. Her fragile, old heart wouldn't take it. If she died and it was his fault, he would live with guilt for the rest of his life. It was true that she was the only person he had. After the death of his father, nobody was as dear to him as his mother, and she defended him against those who mocked him and called him faggot. His mother wouldn't have it. But then again, she would be distraught if she knew the name calling was true.

Fabisiak stood up and headed for the door with tears beginning to roll down his cheeks.

"Oh, we need your photo and fingerprints taken in the room next door, only then, you'll be free to go."

After Fabisiak had left the room, Cegielski dialed the number to the switchboard.

"Put me through to Paprocki, the manager of Teatr Współczesny and tell him this is an urgent matter…"

25TH NOVEMBER 1985
Kamil's flat, Potulicka Street in Szczecin

"Hello, mum, it's me, Kamil. Guess where I'm calling from?"

"Oh, I don't know. Where?"

"From my own flat, they just fitted a landline yesterday!"

"You have no idea how happy I am!" his delighted mother called out.

"I'll come over to yours for dinner on Sunday at around 3:00 p.m. Do you need me to buy anything?"

'No, that's fine.'

"Maybe some ham or sausage, you know, there are way better choices in our departmental shop than in Pewex?" which was a chain of hard currency shops in the People's Republic of Poland that sold otherwise unobtainable Western goods in exchange for Western currencies. Kamil laughed.

"Well, if you could, then, maybe some ham, coffee and a box of chocolate. Aunt Jadźka said she'll be coming over on Tuesday. I'll try to make you something special that you like for dinner. And wait until you see the dessert. But of course, it's a surprise,"

"Sure, I'll get those. See you on Sunday."

"Bye, son."

1ST DECEMBER 1985
Kamil's mother's flat, Szczecin-Załom

While sitting on a passenger train to the station Szczecin-Załom, Kamil was wondering whether he could have still lived here with his mother and commute to work every morning if he didn't have his own flat. An old metal trash bin, all covered with rust, always standing at the entrance to the station and the destroyed bus stop from which the timetable was torn off a long time ago, gave the impression that time had stopped there. Walking across the district of old blocks of flats, he was shocked how he could have lived here for his whole childhood and youthful days. The whole neighborhood and everything in it had looked the same for 20 years. What once seemed familiar and safe, now was old, rotten and obsolete. Now, all this annoyed him and felt strange and unknown. He had hardly any contact with his old friends, too. In fact, he was sure so many of them had forgotten him, but he knew he would never forget them. He still remembered joint crazy bike rallies in the surrounding forest, joint theft of apples from nearby orchards, and summer bonfires at the forest lake. The district of a few grey, four-floor prefabricated blocks located nearby a forest still looked the same.

"My time here is over," he whispered.

When he entered the flat, he kissed his mother and a little cur dog called Mika jumped up happily. Kamil petted the dog caressingly. She licked his hand. He glanced around the room, looking at the timelessness of it all. There was an old Rubin, a make of old, Soviet Union televisions manufactured from 1955 that his father received a ration stamp for in 1979 which stood near the window as it always has. A dark brown table, heavy, theatrical, maroon curtains and a tibial, shiny wall unit and a hazel, rubbed down rug all reminded him of his youth and numerous family parties. Christmas time with his parents and a scented Christmas tree, his first Holy Communion or his 18th birthday, when he got drunk for the first time in his life. When he looked around the room, he saw that nothing really had changed.

"Who would have thought your phone would get fitted this quickly?" his mother rejoiced. "We might not live that far from each other, yet I only get to see you once a month for our Sunday dinner. At least now you can call more often." His mother looked him up and down. She suddenly looked worried. "You don't look good, you've lost weight, what do you even eat?" Her mouth was going a mile a minute. "A female could at least make you a proper dinner," she added, frowning.

"Oh, mum, I already told you that we have a very good departmental canteen." He forced a smile, trying not to look annoyed at her last comment. "I never go hungry."

"Come on, have a sit. Have a sit," she said, patting the seat. It was the same chair made of solid wood with a red quilted pillow on which he used to sit as a child for each meal or to do his homework. The chair was probably as old as he was, and as far as he remembered, it had always been part of the apartment's furniture and always in the same spot.

"I'll bring the soup in. I've made pea soup, just like you like it, with a lot of sausage. And how's work?"

"Same old, same old. Just more documents to work on. Nothing different, for now. I have a few days of training in mid-December in Krakow, and they will probably move me to a different Department after the New Year, but that's nothing certain, yet."

"And what would you have to do?"

"Probably the same thing I do now, but I would get to work outside with people more, because now, I just work with the papers."

"Do you like it?" His mother took his plate and ran to the kitchen. "I'm just getting the pork chops. I made them the way you like them, with a lot of roux and a pickled cucumber on the side." She smiled just before disappearing with Kamil's plate and then reappearing with a delicious, juicy pork chop just the way he liked them. "You just sit there, in that flat of yours, all alone, it's about time you find yourself a woman. Don't you get bored?" she kept on dwelling on the subject.

"No, sometimes I go out for a pint with my colleague after work, and I do volleyball three times a week. On Saturdays, we go out dancing with my team mates to Bosmańska, a restaurant in Szczecin," Kamil embellished the story. He has only been out dancing twice and he didn't like it one little bit. He didn't like going out dancing with his friends. Girls had always found him handsome and were eager to flirt. He never understood it, but when his friends were constantly trying to figure out new ways to pick up girls, he never went out of his way and was somehow more successful than them without putting in much effort. Even when having a nice conversation with a girl, he always felt that she was expecting something more. He never liked the way how, when out drinking, a drunk woman would get angry at him for not wanting something more or being interested in them. He felt uncomfortable and out of place. Once, when he didn't want to go dancing, he told his friend that that wasn't his thing. When he asked what his thing was, Kamil was confused and said nothing, realizing the absurdity of the situation. What man didn't like to dance with a woman?

"And how have you been, Mum?" he changed the subject.

"Well, I'm not that young anymore, and neither is my health. The doctor changed my high blood pressure medicine. *Again.* I thought I would get a chance to play with my grandchildren before I die. Why did you split up with Beatka? I still don't understand? After all, you were together for over three years and she slept over here so many times. I was sure she would be my daughter-in-law. Also, your father liked her before he passed."

"Oh, Mum, just let it go. We weren't good together, so we just split up." This whole talk with his mother began to irritate him a little. He felt the fork slipping from his grasp as his hands became sweaty. Instinctively, he licked his lips and bit his lower lip from the inside so hard that he felt the taste of his own blood on his tongue.

"I ran into her at the market a while ago. She asked how you were. Maybe you could get back with

26

her? You have your own flat now, with a phone, and a good job. If your father was still alive, he would be so proud of you..." It saddened his mother to be without grandchildren. She always saw herself surrounded by a bunch of grandchildren, and always made sure Kamil knew it, especially after her husband's death, she felt increasingly lonely. She often told Kamil that she sometimes talked to Mika just to keep herself busy. The neighbors thought she was an old freak, anyway. She also worried that, because of the sheer volume of work and neglected private life, Kamil might end up an old bachelor.

"I have lots of work now and no time for some marriage business, and you, Mum, you just keep bothering me with it."

"No, I just... I'm just worried. That's all. Wait here. I'll just bring the cheesecake and pack the rest for you to take home, since I won't be able to eat it all myself anyway." His mother drifted between the dining room and the kitchen and back again with the cheesecake. She plopped down a small slice on a small dish in front of him, and the scent of rum and raisins drifted up and into the air.

"Jesus, I love the smell."

"Yes, yes, I added quite a lot of rum and raisins, just like you have always liked."

"Thank you." He smiled, looking at his mother. She has grown a little chubby and you could now see new wrinkles on her face. Her slightly burnt perm and auburn hair dye only gave her more charm. As always, she wore the same, navy dress wrapped in a white apron.

"Does the TV work?" Kamil asked.

"It does. But what do I ever watch? The news and

sometimes a film, because I go to bed early. Good thing I have a dog, at least I don't go on walks alone."

"Mum, have you ever met any homosexuals?" Kamil asked abruptly."

"I don't think I have. Why are you asking?"

"No, I'm just asking because I read some article lately. You know the article was mocking and full of aggression, although I remember from uni courses that many famous writers and poets were also homosexuals."

He felt she believed him but his cheeks turned red anyway.

"Actually, your father once said that Mr. Waldek, the one whose allotment was next to ours, is one of them. In fact, he's never had a wife and I have never seen him with any woman." She became lost in thought. "Also, once, Staszek, your father's friend, said that there was this guy at their shipyard who even wore lipstick, but he didn't stay there for long." She twisted her face in disgust and shook her head. She couldn't understand how a normal, healthy man could behave like that.

"Poor people," she continued. "They should be treated. Although, I remember Mr. Waldek being really friendly and helpful. Oh! I almost forgot. Karolina, the one that lives at number six, the one you went to school with, has just had a baby girl and wanted to ask you if you would agree to be the godfather. Can I give her your number." This took him by surprise. The last time he saw Karolina was over a year ago, at the birthday of a mutual friend of theirs. They spent a lot of time together when they were young, going to church, to first parties, on trips. They used to always visit each other when one of them was ill. But time passed and they went their separate paths. Kamil didn't even realize when it happened.

"Yes, you may give it to her, but I don't want to play these games."

"Oh, come on, you don't say *no* to a child, and besides, it's just a formality. You have only seen your godfather around, what, three times in your life? Think about it"

"That's true."

"And that Andrzej, at number 11, has just had a second baby. His wife gave birth around two months ago, but I forgot to tell you the last time you came. Who would have thought, after all, he's a year younger than you are."

"Ah well, I'll help you clean up and I'll get going, how about that?" Now, he was becoming even more irritated and just wanted to leave.

"Don't worry about it. I'll clean up myself. I don't like people messing with my kitchen. Are you leaving, already? You've only just finished eating," she was surprised.

"Yes, I still have one thing to prepare for tomorrow for work. Here, that's what you asked for: coffee, chocolates and ham"

"Thank you! Such treasures!" She hugged him.

"I'll call you during the week."

Kamil kissed his mother, petted Mika and left the flat quickly. He felt on edge after this whole situation with his mother, but why?

All this constant bullshit about marriage! I deserve a few larger pints, I'm getting pissed tonight!!!

* * *

He decided to get drunk at Piast, the bar nearest to where he lived. The pink walls had long faded from

29

old age, and the wooden purple high tables had scratch marks all over them. At this time of night, the bar was full of drunken men of all ages. Inside it reeked of cigarettes, sweat, and cheap booze. Kamil ordered two pints of beer and a small glass of vodka right away. He stood at a table in the corner and started to think about the evening at his mother's home. Even though he was clearly irritated at first, each sip of alcohol made him more and more relaxed, with the irritation slowly giving way to a state of sweet blissfulness. After the first beer and the vodka, he realized he was looking at the men in the bar differently than usual; checking out their facial features, their bodies, whether they were with any women or not. He glanced around, hoping by some coincidence that the blonde-haired man back at the operation would be here.

Ever since he had seen that man, he would think about him before falling asleep, his blue eyes, his chiseled face. Kamil thought about that situation and had doubts whether it really happened or if it was just his imagination.

He laid his eyes on a young worker in a work uniform, drinking beer with his friends. The man was very rowdy, but he wouldn't't call him say aggressive. He was about 26-27, with jet-black hair, two-day facial hair and slightly protruding ears. He was tall, and he must have been almost 6'1". The worker was already clearly drunk, and his big black eyes glistened like some rabid dog. There was something wild, fascinating and at the same time repulsive about him. He was clearly the leader of his group and everyone paid attention to what he was saying as he barked out a story that Kamil could not hear to a group of friends.

There was something attractive about it to Kamil, something primal and sexy.

Suddenly feeling really drunk, Kamil knew that in another moment and another drink later, he wouldn't be able to get home on his own. He wobbled towards the door and left the bar, trying his best he can to get home safely.

5TH DECEMBER 1985
WUSW building, Małopolska Street in Szczecin

"Hey, you here already? It's not even eight yet!" Robert exclaimed, surprised to see Kamil with a rick of folders stacked into a few separate piles on his desk. They had come in this morning.

"These must be the files from the November 15 action. The people from Mazurska sent them," continued Robert.

"Yeah, I'm early, because I need to take a look through a few files connected to this operation from over two weeks ago," Kamil said, his voice a bit groggy and hung-over from the night before. Robert said nothing of it.

For more than an hour now, Kamil frantically skimmed through all the folders from the 15th of November, when he had completed his task, two weeks ago. Brought over from the police station on Mazurska Street, all the folders were black in color and in the format of A4. Apart from the photo, fingerprints and some basic credentials, there was a short description of a person's personality and appearance and their connections.

The thought of the strange blond guy, whom he had only exchanged a few looks with at the corridor, hasn't given him a break for the past fortnight and

Kamil didn't quite know why. All he knew was that he needed to find out who this man was and where he could find him.

Flipping through a countless stack of folders, he came across the head of the hospital in Pomorzany, a municipal neighborhood of the city of Szczecin, who had treated his mother; moments later, he even found a folder of his primary school teacher, who had taught him Polish.

What would happen, if people found out that literally at every place of work there is something of this kind, he thought for a while.

"And where exactly is on your mind today?" Robert asked bluntly.

Kamil gave Robert a blank look. He needed a while to sober up, collect his bearings. He realized that Robert was starting to suspect something. Well versed in hiding his emotions and feelings, he scratched his forehead and frowned as if he'd lost the count of some numbers in his head. Suddenly his expression became very serious. Trying to appear as professional as possible and looking Robert dead in the eye with a straight face, he said, "No, I've just been thinking, looking through these files, that there are so many *others* in our society. A moment ago, I just found my primary school teacher's folder."

"Have you ever met anyone like that?" he asked.

"I did have a very distant cousin, who quickly became a professional soldier. Unfortunately, after two years in the army, somebody grassed him up and he was fired for his weird tendencies. I know he later left for Krakow and I have lost all touch with him. Besides, it's still a massive secret in our family and a taboo nobody dares to speak of. But that's just for your ears, of course." Kamil wanted to get Robert to trust him, to let him in on something only he was privy to make it seem like Kamil trusted him. But, more importantly, to get Robert off his back.

'I've heard that one guy from Section D on the second floor is also one of them and that he was once caught with another man in a park. Later, his wife divorced him, took his child and ran away. Maybe it's just rumors, I'm not sure. Those people, they don't have it easy, but they bring it upon themselves. You've seen it yourself. Oh, and get this funny story," Robert excitedly slipped in. "One time my wife and I were at the beach in Międzyzdroje, before we had children. My wife went to take a walk down the coast for a bit, but she hadn't come back after a long while, so I began to look for her. I quickly found her talking to some lady. I remember, she was quite fit, long blonde hair. But later I found out that she was a lesbian, because she wanted to take my wife's naked photoshoot at the beach. I'm not sure how that would have ended if I hadn't stepped in in time!" Robert began laughing loudly.

What is like to fall asleep with one person, yet imagine another? Pretending to be something you're not? Is such a life a kind of cowardice or an extraordinary ability to adapt to such situation in order to survive? The thoughts spun his mind into a spiral and gave him a headache.

"And what's up with you?" Robert asked suspiciously.

"What? I'm not upset or anything, just fucking knackered. We pushed it at the workout yesterday and I'm all sore today," Kamil said, managing to quickly stutter up a reasonable excuse.

"Oh, I see." Robert said in a voice so warm and friendly that his tone sent a chill up Kamil's spine. The expression on Robert's face was so false and dishonest, like a humble servant who was about to give a cup of wine with a poisonous cowbane to his emperor.

Despite having skimmed through over 200 personal files he hadn't found the one he was looking for, and there were still over 50 folders left.

"Do you know, if I was to become a godfather, do I have to ask the boss for a permission? He knew that on Communist Poland, the Church was in opposition to the ruling party. Militia officers and their families officially couldn't go to church and be Catholic. They had to ask for permission from their superiors to attend any church ceremonies. The Church cooperated with the countries on the other side of the Iron Curtain and lent support to those persecuted by the communist regime.

"No, you don't need to. Just hand in a written request, justify it properly, saying that these people are your close friends and you cannot refuse or something," Robert answered.

"Well then, are we wrapping up for today? It's almost four. Do you want to grab a pint at Wiarus?" Robert suggested friendlily.

"No, not today, I just want to finish this and go home. I told you I'm dead beat. Besides, I still need to write that request for our boss about being the godfather. Plus, I'm still feeling it from last night."

"Long night, huh?" Robert asked, as he raised an eyebrow.

"Yeah, you can say that."

"Well, I'm not pressing," he drawled out. "I am leaving. I'll see you tomorrow. Oh, the training in

Krakow has been canceled due to organizational difficulties, I forgot to let you know."

Kamil finally let out his breath quietly. He didn't feel like beer and chatting to Robert constantly about the same topics. He kept on looking through the folders, but the one he wanted, he could not find. *"God, 20 more to go."* He was slowly falling into doubt that he could ever find it, but what he had experienced at the station in the corridor was no mirage. Maybe it was somebody very dangerous and his files were transferred to a different division, or maybe they just got lost? When there were only two folders left on his desk, he felt exhausted and disappointed.

So much work, and for what? It was probably tossed into the pile from a different day, he thought. He was just about to leave but decided to give it one last go. When he opened the last folder, Kamil froze. *"That's him!"* The face of the blond, curly haired man with blue eyes stared back at him from the photo.

Name and Surname: Piotr Graczyk
Date of Birth: 7th August 1955
Parents' names: Stanisław, Jadwiga
Age: 30 y.o.
Profession: clergyman (a priest)
Place of work: The Parish of the Sacred Heart 14 Wojska Polskiego Avenue, 71-745 Szczecin.

13TH DECEMBER 1985

Teatr Współczesny in Szczecin, Director Paprocki's Office

"Good morning, director."

"Oh, it's you, Mr. Fabisiak, please come in and have a seat."

Paprocki's office looked like a ballroom. There were photos of performances from the 50's and 60's hung all over the walls. Massive, arched windows with purple curtains long enough to reach the floor and huge, crystal chandeliers reminded him of the past of this historic building. Paprocki sat in a bulky, quilted armchair behind a dark brown, oak, chiseled desk, dressed in a blue jacket. To Fabisiak, he resembled the government inspector from Gogol's play.

"Some tea?" Asked the director, motioning with his hand to a steaming hot tea kettle.

"No, thank you. I've just had coffee."

"How do you find your role of the butler in *Śluby Panieńskie*?"Paprocki asked, getting straight to the point.

"Just another role, director. I try to play my part the best I can," he said. *What is this about?* he thought, cautiously.

"Of course. Nobody doubts that. I'm just asking.

We, here, are very happy with you. You have saved more than one performance," the director laughed.

Theater directors never took Fabisiak seriously as an actor. Still, his talent and extraordinary sense of humor were the two things not even the harshest of critics could deny him. He was second to none when it came to substituting actors who called in sick. Often when a protagonist forgot his or her lines or there were some issues with the stage design, Fabisiak would jump out on the stage and amuse the audience with his improvised comedy bits, playing it off as if it were just part of the play. Quite often after the show they remembered his acting better than that of the protagonists.

You better tell me what you're getting at. I don't trust you.

"I called you in, because we want to get going with a new play, something more for the people, a comedy. Enough of these school books on stage. We need something to attract a full audience on Saturdays and Sundays, not just school trips on weekdays. We need something extra, a performance that's new, fresh, and innovative. Something that will bring people to their knees. At the end of May, in Krakow, they announced this contest for theaters from around the country. If we can make it to the main competition, that would already be quite an achievement for our theater, let alone if we won the main prize.

You have no idea what's going on, on stage or outside of it, after all, you're just another pawn sent by the Ministry of Culture, Fabisiak thought.

"So, that's exactly why I asked you here today," Paprocki carried on. "Do you remember the film from 1973 by Bareja called *Man Woman Wanted?* About that major who was accused of stealing a painting and had to hide dressed as a woman?"

"Sure, I remember. It's one of my favorite movies."

"And how would you see yourself in that role? It would be the leading and the most responsible role. But, after all, such a professional actor with your experience will surely manage."

As if you know anything about my talent, thought Fabisiak and groaned, "Well, I... In fact... well, yes, but..."

"But, Mr. Fabisiak, I don't think there is anything to consider here. You should just try," the director pressed on. "I was thinking about a few people for this role, but most of them will not be able to bear its weight."

What a load of bullshit. All these years you've been ignoring me for the main roles and now, all of a sudden, I'm the best fit? I don't trust you... On the other hand, I've got nothing to lose.

"Please, think about it and let me know tomorrow."

"I will, director," coughed up Fabisiak, a little surprised with how things turned out. "Well, I mean..." he hesitated. "I've already decided. I'll take the role."

"Well, Mr. Fabisiak, well done for your quick, manly decision," the director said shaking his hand. "The rehearsals begin on Monday."

"Thank you, director, I promise I'll do my best on stage."

Oh hell, I'll finally show them all!

"I have no doubts about that," the director smiled ironically.

5TH JANUARY 1986

Kamil was just frying his black pudding. He was wondering why so many people don't like it. *"Is it because it's made out of blood?"* He could eat it, fried in a pan with onions, every day.

His phone rang and snapped him out of his thoughts.

"Hallo? Kamil?"

"Yes."

"Hi. It's Karolina here, from your primary school. Your mum gave me this number and said I could call." Her voice shook nervously for a moment.

"Oh, hi. It's you. I'm glad you've called. Congratulations on your baby girl. What's her name, and how have you been?"

"Thanks, she was born a month ago and her name's Emilka."

"That's great, she's probably got her mum's looks."

"Aw, Kamil, you flatterer," Karolina laughed. Her voice steadied. As she spoke of her child, she sounded calmer, happier, but also excited "Well, you probably already know why I'm calling."

"Yeah, Mum mentioned something."

"Edek and I would like to ask you to become the godfather of our baby. I thought of you, because we grew up together and we have always been like brother and sister. If you say no, we'll understand. Don't worry."

He hoped Karolina would forget and not call. He never considered himself a Catholic, and he took his First Communion at nine only because his grandmother insisted. The few church ceremonies he had to take part in were frowned upon at work and in the ZSMP. Not only that, every visit to the church was a somewhat stressful experience. He never knew any of the prayers by heart and had no idea when to stand up or kneel down.

When Karolina phoned, his initial reaction was to turn her down, but that would have been very cruel of him after all they had been through. They'd seen too many things together. He thought back to that one time in second grade when they went to the woods to pick up mushrooms without telling their parents. They got lost there and it took them five hours to find their way home, only to find that their parents had already notified the militia. After that incident, they were both grounded from watching TV for two months. Another memory from his childhood that he cherished was him teaching Karolina how to hold her breath under water in the tub in her bathroom, after which they flooded the floor downstairs. They had known each other too long for him to say no now, and Karolina was too worried and happy with becoming a mother.

"No, why? I'm happy you've asked. Sure, I'll be happy to be her godfather," Kamil drawled, trying to sound pleasant. "When and where is the Christening?"

"On the 18th of January at 10:00. Saint Mateusz Church on Pocztowa Street, because it's Edek's parish."

"Yeah, sure, I'll be there."

"Remember to get a certificate from your parish to confirm that you're a Roman Catholic. It's important."

"Consider it done. I'll try to get there early, by 9:30 a.m."

"Thank you, Kamil."

Kamil took a breath of relief. Lucky it's not the Parish of the Sacred Heart. *I don't think I would even know how to act if I saw the stranger Piotr at the altar,* he laughed quietly to himself.

18TH JANUARY 1986
Saint Mateusz Church, Pocztowa Street in Szczecin

Kamil got to the church at quarter past nine. It was a cold day. It was snowing abundantly, and the wind made the snowflakes stick directly to Kamil's face. Shoe traces left in the snow vanished within a matter of seconds. Kamil, wearing a thick black leather jacket with a white sheepskin collar, gray cotton trousers and black leather boots, began to pace to get some heat and warm up. Numerous families and their guests gathered at the church's gate. The church was quite big and looked like a 16th century building—narrow, perpendicular windows and red brick pointed to late gothic. The shape of the tower reminded him of a Soviet Pershing missile he had seen in a newspaper. The crowd at the church was growing larger by the minute. Further taxies and private cars pulled up: Polonezes, the Polish Fiat 125p, Volgas and Skodas. People poured out of them and into the street.

"There you are!" Karolina shouted from behind, surprising Kamil.

Karolina and Edek looked like a typical married couple in their twenties working their way up: she—a slim, dinky blond working at a kindergarten, he— ginger, tall and slightly alienated. He was a team leader of one of the production lines in Polmo in Szczecin. He thought they were good together even though he hardly knew the two of them together. But, after all, they've been a couple for four years.

"Hi. Wow! Hi, how are you? Why, you haven't changed at all! My God, how long has it been?" Kamil said. He kissed Karolina and then greeted Edek with a firm handshake.

"I haven't seen you in so long." Karolina continued. Karolina pushed a large black, big-wheeled pram, but it was hard to force it through the snow. Inside the pram was a tiny baby wrapped in various layers of baby clothes and blankets, so much that only a small head in a blue cap could be seen. The child was asleep. Although Kamil didn't like children, he had to admit that the little girl was cute and bore some resemblance to Karolina.

"What a beautiful, little princess," Kamil choked up seeing the child, pretending to be the good uncle.

"We haven't seen each other for so long. How have you been, Kamil? I heard you got an apartment in Szczecin. Where do you live now?"

"Yes, it's true," answered Kamil, glad that Karolina wasn't asking about his private life for now. "I live in a residential district on Potulicka, which is also close to where I work."

"That's great, congratulations," she replied. "I hope you'll be soon inviting us to see *your* kid baptized, won't you?" She wouldn't let go, trying to find out if Kamil had a girlfriend.

Why are women so curious? he asked himself.

"I don't think it will be *that* soon," answered Kamil looking around and nervously laughing. "I think we'd better get inside. It's getting crowded."

The entrance to the church consisted of two 2.5-meter-long wooden, brown, heavy oak doors. Old brass door handles complemented the chic design. Walking down the granite gray stairs sprinkled with sand, Kamil helped Karolina with the pram. The room was almost full. It was warm inside the church, clearly warmer than outside. Colorful stained glass in the windows with different representations of saints reminded Kamil of his First Communion.

Kamil took a sneak peek to look at the people around him. Most of the women were wearing nutria fur coats, which were considered a higher social status. The men looked more classical and uniform, similar, black or brown coats and jackets, creased trousers and polished shoes.

Most of the people were sneezing or coughing, a sign of a brutal winter this year. Kamil hasn't felt the church atmosphere for a long time. His father, a diehard communist, forbade him from attending the sacrament of confirmation. He felt strange here, but he enjoyed the feeling of calmness and respite.

The altar was decorated in white orchids, whose perfume spread all over the church. There were two, big candles lit up at the sides of the altar, with two smaller, yellow ones below.

"When will you invite us to your wedding and a Christening after?" Karolina whispered.

"Not anytime soon. You know, nobody wants a guy like me," Kamil said, trying to turn it into a joke.

Karolina laughed quietly. "Stop it! The girls in our class have always said you were so handsome, just so… unavailable. Anyway. So, how's work?"

"You know, the work of an official is not a piece of

cake. You are constantly bombarded with mountains of paperwork, annoying bosses, and exhausting hours, it's tedious, but it pays the bills. Nothing exciting, really."

Exactly at 10:00 somebody began playing the pipe organ, interrupting their side conversation. Everyone stood. A priest came out from the room at the back. Kamil didn't pay any attention to him, but when he looked closer, he nearly leaped out of the pew. It was Piotr Graczyk, whom he met before at the corridor at the police station. He wore a white Alb and asked all the parents to queue up.

The christening ceremony itself went smoothly and, soon after, the service began. But Kamil paid no attention. He found his eyes completely locked on to Piotr's blue ones the entire time. He couldn't believe he was seeing Piotr again.

What is this about? He was supposed to be working for a different parish

During the service, after Piotr read a few lines from the Old Testament—The Letter to the Romans by Apostle Paul—he looked up from the pages to Kamil and their eyes met again. Kamil quickly turned his head away abashed, but after a short moment, it happened again. Kamil's heart almost popped out.

"Kamil, what's wrong with you?" Karolina asked.

"Me? Nothing. It's hot in here," he lied as he tugged at the collar of his dress shirt.

But Karolina did not give up so easily.

"Do you know this priest?" she asked, whispering.

"No, why?" His voice shook. Kamil wished the Earth would swallow him up.

"Just asking, because he keeps on staring at you strangely. Have you met before?"

Kamil almost started to stutter. His heart began to pound, and his face turned red.

"Kamil, did you hear what I said? Are you okay?"

"No, I don't think so. Maybe he knows me from my volleyball matches? I don't know." His hands got wet from the sweat and chills went through his body. His mouth dried up, too, as if he hadn't had a drop of water for days. When he tried to answer Karolina, he couldn't articulate his thoughts. Instinctively, he grabbed the button of his jacket and began to twist it so much to one side that he almost pulled it out.

Karolina's child began to cry. She turned away from Kamil and tried to hush her daughter. She leaned over the pram and picked up the baby. While she was rocking her, Edek put the teat in the baby's mouth and stroked her forehead. After a while the child calmed down and Karolina put her back in the pram.

For the rest of the service, Kamil stared down at the floor, afraid that if he looked at Piotr again, he would faint. When they left the church, he felt his senses returning to him. He wiped his sweaty palms on his pants and took in a breath.

After the service, everyone piled into three cars and headed off to a celebration dinner at Edek's home. In the car on their way back, Kamil told Karolina that he probably has met this priest in one of the matches for sure, in an attempt to get rid of any suspicion she may have thought his encounter with the priest was something more... intimate.

Isn't this whole meeting today some kind of fate?

Most of the evening Kamil tried to avoid Karolina. If Karolina was nearby, he would either go out to the kitchen or pretend to be busy talking with

47

other guests. He drank vodka glass by glass, and discussed with Edek about his work, sports or recent events. The party at Edek's and Karolina's home finished late at night after 2:00 a.m. in the morning. After Kamil had a few shots of vodka, he felt his nerves subsiding. But just as a precaution, Kamil avoided Karolina for the rest of the night

21ST JANUARY 1986

Today was a hard day at work, a bunch of phone calls and reports. It was almost dark when Kamil set off for home, exhausted. On his way to his studio, he stopped by a bookstore window at the corner of the street. The salesman was just putting up the latest volume of the *Tytus, Romek i A'Tomek,* the longest-published and one of the most popular Polish comic book *s*eries. He rushed into the bookstore and bought the latest episode. Ever since he could remember, he has always been slightly crazy about these comic books. They reminded him of his childhood, and, to this day, he has been collecting them. He walked home so happy, as if carrying a true treasure under his arm.

Walking down his block, he took a letter out of his mailbox. He opened a bottle of his favorite Polo-Cockta, Poland's answer to Coca Cola, and only now realized there was a stamp at the corner of the envelope. It read: St. Mateusz Parish. He quickly opened it and started reading.

Dear Sir,
We kindly ask you to visit our parish as soon as possible in order to complete the missing documentation on the christening of Emilia Zbytkowska, daughter of

Edward and Karolina, which took place on 18th January, 1986. The parish is open Monday to Saturday from 8:00 A.M. till 4:00 P.M.

> *Yours Sincerely,*
> *Pastor Maciej Zięba*

His stomach twisted in nervousness and fluttered with excited butterflies at the same time. Did the inglorious Piotr wish to see him again? Was that so? Or is it just a simple oversight and he really did forget to sign some "godfather" form? He decided to call work in the morning and let them know he would be coming in late, so that he could go to the church as soon as possible.

At night, it took him a long time to fall asleep, as he kept on imagining new scenarios of what may happen tomorrow. First, he thought that Piotr wanted to lure him to his parish to get to know him better. *Could it be that he feels and experiences all this the same way I do? Is it even possible? Or maybe I misinterpreted his body language?*

He stood up for a moment and opened the window wide. He took three deep breaths and calmed himself down a bit. Then he went back to bed.

Tomorrow I'll be frank, straightforward and blunt, he decided. *If the formalities can't be dealt with, I'll blame it on them and say I had to take days off work, and that this is completely unacceptable. And what will he do if he sees Piotr tomorrow and they're alone? After all, it could be a trap. Maybe the people from his department are putting him to the test.* The more he thought about it, the more he dismissed that as ridiculous. He was being paranoid and he knew it. He finally calmed down enough to convince himself that the following day would definitely go well. In two days he'll be laughing at himself for even thinking about such ridiculous circumstances.

22ND JANUARY 1986

In the morning, as soon as he woke up, he couldn't get out of bed. Yet again, he dreamt of a situation from his childhood. When he was 13 years old, his parents left him at his aunt's house for a longer period of time during the holidays. He would spend all his time at a city swimming pool called Gontynka, where he met a boy his age, whom he became great friends with. They would play and swim together every day.

On waterslides, Kamil would always sit at the front and Marek would wrap his arms round him from behind. Kamil remembered that the boy always used to hold on to his legs tightly. Marek's touch would send a spike of pleasure through his body. They loved their games, and Kamil quickly realized that Marek had become someone special for him.

One time, when they wrestled on the grass for fun, Kamil rubbed his whole body against Marek's so that Marek lay under him, unable to escape. Marek pretended that he could not free himself and they stayed in that position for a long time. When they finally separated, Kamil knew that they both felt the same inexplicable pleasure. All they did was look into each other's eyes, with no need for words.

Unfortunately, Marek soon left, because he had

only stayed in Szczecin for the holidays. The boys never got a chance to exchange addresses and they lost touch with each other.

Ever since then, Kamil would get the same dream, a few times a year, about him going down a waterslide with Marek and holding his legs tightly.

When Kamil stepped out of his bed, he felt an uncomfortable wetness between his thighs. When he glanced down, he realized he had ejaculated all over his pajamas. He turned on the radio and began to prepare breakfast, as always, two sandwiches with paprykarz szczeciński.

After changing his underwear, he lay down on the bed for a while. He wondered how many times in his life he'd had the same dream. Twenty maybe? And ever since he could remember that dream had always made him wet his pajamas in his sleep. Sometimes he felt guilty thinking that it might be the early signs of some horrible mental disorder. Other times, he wanted to have that dream every night, but the more he thought about it before falling asleep, the more he dreamed of nothing.' *Malinowy król, malowany król [Eng. Raspberry king, painted king],*' Urszula sang in the morning programme on channel three.

'*Czy nie znałam cię w innym życiu już kiedyś hen dawno tak...[Eng. Didn't I know you in another life? Long, long time ago...]*'

I like this song more every day, he thought.

It took him a long time to choose what to wear. Finally, he decided to go for casual—brown, creased trousers and a blue shirt with a blazer, coat and a flat cap to cover his head. *After all, I have to go to work afterwards,* he summed up. Before leaving, he sprinkled his neck with his favorite cologne called Wiarus. He rushed it to the church on foot. He didn't feel like waiting at a tram stop, and he feared that public transit could be suffering delays after the heavy snowfall. He walked briskly.

Overnight, it had snowed again, covering the whole city in a white layer of shiny fluff.

When he got to his destination, he knocked on the sacristy door. An elderly woman wearing a babushka opened it.

"Good morning, my name is Kamil Adamski, I received a letter from you asking me to report here to fill in some documents."

The woman let Kamil in.

"There, the door on the left." She pointed with a bony finger.

Kamil went over and daintily knocked on the door.

"Come in," a familiar voice answered.

Recognizing the voice immediately, Kamil's heart began to race. When he opened the door, he saw the now familiar stranger—Piotr, dressed in a black soutane—sitting in a small church office room with a huge book laid on his desk. The room smelled of incense.

The church office was small and used to receive visitors. Cream-colored curtains hung in the window and two small round cacti with white spines stood in brown pots on the windowsill. Because of the white walls, the office appeared to be larger than it actually was. On the wall above the desk hung a large black wooden cross with a silver figure of the crucified Christ, and under it there was a white plastic rosary.

The side walls were adorned with small colorful pictures of different saints. A large desk made of light pine and two identical wooden chairs were the only furniture in the room, except for the green carpet. The desk was kept ascetically neat and tidy. There was a large black plastic telephone on the right corner of the desk. On the other side, a long, half-meter thick white candle was burning, while the center of the desk was occupied by a large, brown, heavy parish book.

"Praised be," said Kamil, his voice shaking. "I got a letter from here, asking me to report in order to fill in some missing documents."

"Have a seat, please," Piotr smiled a little secretly. Piotr, gently took the letter from Kamil's hand. His body language was very composed, and his face—very focused. His act was very official.

"Oh, it's you," he looked at something in his great book for a moment. "No, that would be a mistake, someone must have missed the faith statement you have submitted, but I do now see it right here, with all the other documents. It's in the files," he said in a low husky voice.

"Would you like a drink? It's freezing today," Piotr surprised Kamil with his offer.

"No... Or, actually, could I get some tea, please?" Kamil answered. Although he saw the chair and Piotr brewing a pot of tea, he was too nervous and worried about the whole situation to sit down. It all happened too fast. He didn't know if it would be better to stay or just run away. It seemed like there was a magical force at work that didn't want to let him leave.

"Sure, I'll just get that for you," Piotr poured water into a clay kettle and plugged it in.

55

An awkward silence filled the room for a while.

"I won't stay long, otherwise I'd be late for work," Kamil said smiling.

"And where do you work, if I may ask?"

"I'm a state official. You know, pastor, working on documents and calculating the statistics. And you, pastor, you also probably have a lot of work, all the christenings, weddings, funerals."

"Please, call me Piotr," he said reaching to shake Kamil's hand.

"Kamil, pleasure."

Their handshake lasted longer, as if neither of them wanted to let go, and they kept on staring into each other's eyes.

Kamil felt strangely absorbed and dizzy with the whole situation. He wanted to stay in the moment forever. He had the impression that he had already felt that special feeling before, but it had been a long time ago, probably during a memorable vacation when he met Marek from the last dream. It seemed as if he had been waiting for this state of mind and body for years, but nothing would ever happen. When it finally did, he felt no embarrassment or shame. He was ready to give in to his emotions without fighting them, come what may.

"Please have a seat," offered Piotr, pointing at one of the chairs.

Finally, when they sat down, Kamil asked, "and you, Piotr, have you been working here for long?" He didn't know he was capable of such courage—easing his discomfort and allowing himself to relax.

"No. Only for a month, this isn't my parish. One of the priests here left for a seminar to Rome and I'm substituting for him until the end of July."

Right, that's all clear now, you're not in the Parish of the Sacred Heart, he thought.

"And what do priests do after work? Do they even have any free time?" he asked boldly.

"They live like anyone else. I go swimming twice a week, I read books, and I'm planning on going to the cinema."

"Oh, the cinema," Kamil picked up quickly. He perked up an eyebrow out of interest. "To see what?"

"The film called *Alabama,* one with Urszula, Polish pop and rock singer.

"Actually, I was going to go see it, too," Kamil smiled looking him straight in the eye.

"Why not go together?" replied Piotr with a slight smirk on his face and casually shrugging his shoulders. "The film is on at Kosmos at six."

"I'll get there early and buy the tickets," Kamil offered. Kamil's body was filled with joy. His hands on the table were literally jumping with excitement and his legs could foxtrot right there. If he could, he would climb up the chair and scream: Finally! But instead he kept composed, kept his legs and his hands steady as best he could, and then exchanged a small nod toward Piotr.

"That's fine. So, we're good?"

"Yeah! I'll get going now," said Kamil, again reaching to shake Piotr's hand.

"Thank you for coming." Piotr squeezed Kamil's hand tightly.

"But weren't you in a hurry to get to work?" Piotr asked with a sly smile.

They would have remained in this little sexy game much longer if it wasn't for someone knocking on the door. They jumped right off each other, and the woman with the babushka on her head walked in.

"Well, goodbye, pastor," Kamil coughed up, choking on laughter.

"God bless!" answered Piotr with a hint of a smile.

* * *

Walking to work, Kamil felt all the joys of spring. *On Saturday, I'm going to the cinema with a priest!* Only now, did he realize the absurdity of this whole situation. The church and priests who almost openly supported the underground and fought with the security apparatus, and he an SB officer, who after work arranges a date for the cinema with a priest. It looked as if Reagan privately arranged with Gorbachev for a beer at a pub on Saturday evening.

Frosty Szczecin looked so beautiful and the sun, which now came out, reflected off the snow blinding people. He was so happy and excited that he wanted to go for a long walk in the park or forest to rethink again what had happened. He remembered how he had once found 100 zlotys on the sidewalk on his way to school. After finding the 100 zlotys he then decided to ditch school and spend all the money on the amusement park. It was one of those secret and happy days that he never told anyone about and that he would remember forever.

That's how he felt now, like an innocent schoolboy who wanted to skip out on work because he had a date. Unfortunately, he was now in front of the building where he worked. It was for him the last place he wanted to spend the rest of the day. When he got to work, he began to regret not having taken the day off.

"What's up with you?" Robert greeted him in a harsh voice from behind the desk. "Won the jackpot?"

"Me? No. Why?" Kamil asked abashed. Though, he felt like he had.

"Your face is all happy, smiling, your eyes glistening. Have you met some chick, or what?" Robert kept asking.

"No, I don't feel too well, I think I've got a cold and a fever, to be honest," Kamil lied.

Kamil quickly sat at his desk and pretended to be setting up his work. He tried to focus on the documents, but his thoughts were occupied with one thing only. *Looks like I have a date,* he smiled to himself. *But how can I, for fucks sake, wait until Saturday!?*

Hey, maybe we can get a beer today after work since you seem so chipper and full of energy. Afterall, the second time is not refused."

Robert made a face of a sweet bear from the shop window.

Kamil, smiling, pretended for a moment that he was thinking about the offer. "You know, I think I'll take you up on that offer." Kamil replied and then they both laughed, exchanging knowing looks.

* * *

The cheap Wiarus bar was not full late in the middle of the week. Several tables were occupied by permanent bums, and the rest of the local drunks were just beginning to descend. Old images of famous places of Szczecin hung on the blue walls. There were

20 tables inside with pink-green plastic oilcloths and white-wood-metal chairs. The dim light from old glass chandeliers and the slippery gray granite floor were making this place look like a typical dive, one of many such places in this city. Robert started the round, bringing two beers and two vodkas from the bar which he put on the table.

"Jesus, man," started Robert. He took up the beer and tipped it to his lips, nearly chugging half the pint down. "Enjoy being single. A grumpy wife and two children can give you a hard time."

"My great respect for your wife that she can manage it all," said Kamil.

"It's a fact," admitted Robert. "Her constant checking up on me, calling the office to ask where I've been, what time will I come back, that I am not helping her. That sometimes drives me crazy."

"The most important thing is that you have a happy family and healthy kids."

"Yes, you are absolutely right. I guess." Robert paused for a moment. "Although my Adam is now five years old, from what I see, he prefers to play with his three-year-old sister's dolls, not with blocks or cars." For a moment in Robert's voice one could feel a slight concern and a tone of slight disappointment."

It's probably normal at this age. He'll probably grow out of it," Kamil retorted.

"I don't know if it's normal. I don't remember ever having a doll in my hand. It was always toy soldiers and cars and blocks for me. That's what we used to do back in the day, before we had all this... gay shit." Robert replied in an icy voice. "I hope it's just a phase. Or I'll have to teach him how to be a true man..."

"What do you mean?" Kamil asked curiously.

"You know..." Robert was confused. "Hmm, I'll have to explain to him that normal boys only play with blocks and cars, and that dolls are only for fags." Kamil frowned in disgust at Robert. "But Julia... Julia is the sweetest child in the world. She is Daddy's favorite daughter." He squealed with joy.

"Do you sit in bed with them in the evenings and read them fairy tales? You know, to help them fall asleep? I remember how much I enjoyed those times as a kid."

"And when the fuck should I do it?" Robert spat out. "It's always work, home, work, home. Never ending. And then on weekends I still have to help in-laws building a summerhouse on their allotment. It's a miracle that I got out with you for a beer today. Well, we're just talking about me, and you, are you going to go through the life alone being a bachelor?" Robert sneered.

"Hmm, I'm looking around for now and I don't think I have found the right person." Kamil casually shrugged and took a swig of his beer.

"The right person?" Robert laughed. "'Are you dating someone now?"

Robert leaned forward, a little too close than Kamil would like. There was the smell of beer, vodka, and just plain old stank slipping from between his lips. With the stench and the two moles on Robert's face, Kamil nearly spat out his beer all over Robert's face. But Kamil kept his lips tight as he swallowed the beer.

"Yes, I have someone, but it's nothing serious." said Kamil, finally. He placed his beer down on the table, and gave a gentle nod. "She's a nurse from the hospital on Arkonska St." He kept his eyes on Robert trying hard not to take them away. If he did, Robert might just think Kamil was lying.

"Oh, really? That's something. And what's her name?" Robert asked.

"Magda." Kamil quickly and confidently replied, giving Robert the details of a former colleague who works there as a nurse. He had been ready for this, preparing it in his head throughout the entire day just for this very scenario. It had to work somehow, because so far none of Kamil's friends knew anything, or at least he thought so.

"Wait one moment." Robert interrupted with a wag of his finger. "I have to go to the toilet."

"OK. Go. Go. Before you piss yourself here," said Kamil. "And I'm going to get another beer and something stronger in the mean time." Kamil stood up from his chair, his feet swaying. Sure, the beer and vodka wasn't strong enough just yet, but something with a little more punch would surely knock him off his feet right now. That he didn't mind just to get through the rest of the work week.

Approaching the bar, he smiled slightly at the barmaid.

"The next two? Or I can give you four straight-away?" A young red-haired bartender in her twenties said to Kamil. Her long hair was so red that it imitated gold glistening in the yellow light of lamps. Pouring beer for Kamil, she smiled licentiously and boldly raised her large round breasts towards him, both of which were nearly slipping out from her purple blouse. Kamil felt a bit confused and he began to blush. It was not the first such situation in his life that he was so shamelessly and indecently picked up by a woman.

"Yes." He answered with a charmer's face, flashing a coy smile for extra effect. "Only two and two vodkas for now so that I can see you again in a moment." He finished off with a wink. The barmaid just laughed bluffly, and she winked back at Kamil. Her pale freckled face and purple lips of the same color as the blouse made her look like a perfectly made porcelain doll. Kamil just smiled and returned to the table.

Robert was sitting at the table clearly agitated and clearly tipsy.

"Fuck! Can you believe this?" He screamed at Kamil, slurring his words "I was pissing myself in the toilet by the wall and here suddenly the guy standing next to me waves his johnson standing in my direction and extends his hand to my cock!"

"What are you talking about?" Kamil stammered out, utterly taken back by the situation. "And what did you do?"

"How? What? Well I smashed him in the mouth of course! Knocked him straight into the wall. I could not finish peeing with a faggot lying there, so I ran out of the bathroom." Robert yelled, waving his arms from side to side. "We have to arrest him for this behavior. He looked drunk out of his mind. Who knows what else he'd do if he got out from the bar and into the streets?"

"No, wait!" Kamil protested. "I'll go there to see if he is still there. I will try to check his identity. Have a beer and stay here because you will do something stupid." Kamil said firmly.

He pretended to be brave when going to the toilet. Drunk alcohol did not help him at all. His heart was pounding. He was most afraid that he would meet Piotr there.

Opening the door slowly, he entered quietly. There were only two toilet cubicles, thankfully empty. He breathed a sigh of relief. Inside, it stank of urine and a strong disinfectant. It was definitely the last place where he could meet Piotr. He washed his face with cold tap water, dried it with the toilet paper, looked in the mirror and returned boldly to the table.

"And what, and what?" Robert asked, being on tenterhooks.

"Nobody is there anymore." Kamil said, pleased, as he came back to the table. "But in fact the blood remains on the floor. Come on, man, some old peasant drank too much and he flipped out."

"Old? Are you joking. He was only about 30 years old." Robert yelled.

"Really?" Kamil looked thoughtful, seeing in his mind himself in that toilet just minutes ago.

"I am not surprised that we organize such actions with those perverts. Look, there is so much of that shit everywhere." Robert continued, annoyed.

"It's all water under the bridge. We didn't come here to get upset and arrest people. We came here to unwind."

"Cheers!' Kamil said raising a glass of vodka. Robert did the same. The burning taste of vodka pleasantly irritated their throats as they threw a swig down into their throats.

"More of the same, please!" Kamil shouted to a waitress who was passing by. After two more glasses of vodka Robert markedly calmed down. After half an hour of idle talk with Kamil about sports and cars, Robert couldn't remember anything about the incident that had happened to him in the toilet. They left the bar well before midnight, staggering and supporting one another. Robert managed to catch a taxi home, and Kamil, walking unsteadily after midnight, reached his apartment.

25TH JANUARY 1986 - SATURDAY

For the whole day at work, Kamil couldn't focus one bit. He didn't pay attention to anything he did. He would nervously peek at his watch and count the minutes to six. And just as the clock struck six, he leaped from his desk, ran home and took a shower to get ready for his very special date.

Good thing I worked out and went to the barber's yesterday, he thought. *I'm glad I had my hair cut the day before.* He always got the same haircut. The sides and back were always trimmed short and the top was kept a little longer. Even though the natural color of his hair was brown, it always seemed jet black to him when he styled it with gel. He shaved his face clean and patted on the after-shave cream. *God, I'm so pale. I could use a little tan.* Unfortunately, now, in the middle of winter, it was wishful thinking. Ever since he remembered, he had always been absolutely crazy about summertime and sunshine, and his skin quickly turned dark brown. He had a dark skin complexion, after his parents. One time, when on vacation by the sea with his mother and father, they joked that they looked like a gypsy family. He looked at his body in the mirror for the last time. Overall, he was pleased with his athletic look, but he knew that his good shape was only the result of exercising frequently. He hoped Piotr would like it.

He decided to wear jeans, which he bought in a resale shop, and a maroon flannel shirt, his favorite, and one he believed he looked best in.

Although the cinema was only 10 minutes walking from his place, he left the house at 4:50 p.m. It was already dark and the evening was frosty, somewhere around three degrees below zero. Despite the relative cold, it was still very pleasant outside because there was no wind. He walked slowly looking at the store windows. The store lights reflected off white snow so that the city shimmered with a somewhat different palette of shades. Reaching the cinema, he noticed in one of the windows a large box of coconut chocolates with a poorly designed photo of the beach and palm trees. He stopped and, staring at the picture, dreamed of being there if only for a while. Holidays in an exotic destination have always been high up on his bucket list, but chances are he will never be able to afford them. While he stood thoughtfully outside the store window, a passerby ran into him. That brought him back from his daydreaming, and he quickly resumed his stroll towards the cinema.

Kosmos was the largest post-war cinema in Szczecin. More and more people were gathering at the entrance. The audience was mostly young mixed couples.

At exactly a quarter past five, he bought two tickets for the back row and impatiently waited in the cinema's hall. It was dark and cold outside, and it started snowing again. At around quarter to six he saw Piotr standing outside. He was wearing a black, polyamide, quilted coat, blue jeans and grey, Relaks boots, a popular and only brand of Polish sports boots, which were very hard to get your hands on. They were insulated with sponge and looked like Western ski boots.

He also wore a navy skiing hat on his head.

"Hi! Kamil rushed to him.

"Oh, hi!" slightly surprised Piotr answered.

They both took their gloves off and shook hands looking deep into each other's eyes. Then, realizing they were in public, they quickly slipped their hands away. Kamil shoved his in his pocket, and Piotr awkwardly shuffled his to his sides.

"Have you been waiting long?" Piotr asked.

"No, around 10 minutes. I was just inside," Kamil lied.

They came in and headed straight for the screening room.

"The back row?" Piotr asked a little surprised, with a hint of a smirk at the edge of his lips.

"Yeah, it has the best view," Kamil answered confidently.

The film had been released for over a month, so the theatre was practically empty. Apart from Kamil and Piotr there were only two more couples in the back row. Piotr wore a brown, V-neck sweater and a grey shirt underneath. He smelled of refreshing cologne, one Kamil was not familiar with.

"How was your day?" Piotr asked.

"I worked out yesterday, and work is just the same as always. A few days ago, I managed to buy *Malinowy Król* by Urszula, so I'm prepared for today," Kamil laughed.

"I've been listening to this album for over two

months now. What's your favorite song?" Piotr asked.
"'I think it's *Twoje zdrowie mała*' Kamil replied.

"Ha, ha, ha, just like mine," Piotr cackled. "I have also lately fell in love with Madonna and I managed to get her cassette in Leszek. My old Grundig is barely working. Have you seen her in the charts on Channel 2?" Kamil asked.

"Yeah, I have 'in that pink dress.' It was in *Material Girl*, or something like that. She truly is amazing. Apparently, the whole of America is crazy about her now," Piotr said.

"No wonder, those magnetic eyes of hers... she really knows how to draw attention to herself. So, what have you been up to since I last got to see you?" Kamil asked.

"Exactly what a priest should be up to..." Piotr smiled mysteriously, revealing his white teeth and piercing Kamil with his glittering eyes.

"I held three masses in our church. In the afternoon, I received parishioners."

"How many times a week do you have to do this?" Asked Kamil.

"Three to four times a week, on average. I like it because people come to me with different problems. A poor old lady once asked if we could hold mass for her late husband and said she would pay me next week when she gets her pension money. And since we know her situation, I said that we would do it free of charge. Aside from that, I taught a religion class to children from a nearby school."

"Oh, quite the busy man, I see?"

The room filled with darkness as the lights dimmed out. The Polska Kronika Filmowa came on.

Kamil tried to focus on the movie, but about 30 minutes in, he found himself glancing over at Piotr every few seconds, trying to steal a glimpse of his beautiful face.

At one point, their eyes met as they both turned to steal a quick look at the other. Kamil wanted to look away, but he couldn't. And neither did Piotr. Kamil slowly inched his legs wider apart, pretending it was a casual and unintentional move. His knee lightly brushed Piotr's knee. After a brief moment, Piotr did the same, touching Kamil's knee harder.

Kamil's penis stirred, coming to attention as it hardened at the sudden warmth of Piotr's knee.

Please, let this moment last forever, Kamil thought. For the first time in his life, he felt pleasantly excited.

His penis was now painfully hard. He wanted to reach out and grab Piotr's groin. He wanted to feel, in between his fingers, Piotr's cock reach full length. He wanted to jerk Piotr's cock till he came in his pants; wanted to be the reason for the stain in his pants and the worry of covering that stain as they walked out of the cinema. But Kamil wouldn't. No, he couldn't. Kamil was a state officer, and Piotr a priest. So Kamil refrained, waited.

After another 20 minutes of the film, Kamil delicately put his hand on the seat's armrest. Piotr clearly moved closer to him, pushing his knee against Kami's even harder. Kamil smirked, trying to keep his eyes on the screen. And yet he understood Piotr's gesture. Kamil dropped his hand onto Piotr's hand resting on the armrest. Their hands finally met. They squeezed each other so hard, as if two hands longing for intimacy have met for the first time in their lives. Blood pumped in their veins like crazy. Kamil glanced down at Piotr's crotch and saw an erection. Both of them were so hard.

At one point, Kamil looked at Piotr, who returned the look. Their eyes glistened with pure fire, lust and the hunger of love. No words were necessary. They froze in this brotherly, tight hold, like a pair of mythical lover—Apollo and Hyacinth.

Just as the film was coming to an end, during the final scene, Kamil could no longer resist the pressure. He turned his head towards Piotr and pressed his lips against Piotr's. Kamil, slipping his fingers through Piotr's hair, grabbed hold of his head and pushed their lips closer together. With a fire burning through them and a newfound confidence, he took hold of Piotr's throbbing penis. Piotr's penis also throbbed like crazy, stretching his trousers.

Piotr did the same. He pressed his hand tightly against Kamil's zipper. Kamil's penis was pulsating like a wild volcano ready to erupt. The feeling of his hand pressed against him and sliding down along with the zipper made Kamil ejaculate harder than he ever had before. The semen nearly broke through his underwear. His body literally jumped on the chair from the sudden pleasure that his new friend had just given him. He had never expected that, in the right context and with the right person, he could reach the peak of stimulation in such an inconspicuous place as a movie theater.

Final credits appeared on the screen. First the only other couple in the theater got up and left. That made them realize the film was over. Only now did they move apart. For a while they just sat there without looking at each other, gasping for breath. They still couldn't believe what had just happened.

The lights came on and they indolently stood up from their seats and put on their coats. Kamil felt his knickers were soaked through and sticky. When they were leaving the cinema, he admitted to himself that he hadn't been this happy in a very long time.

"How did you like the film?" Kamil asked as they stepped out of the building and into the cold, snowy air.

"It was good, and the music too, Urszula is in great shape... and generally, the whole performance was amazing, thanks to my new friend," Piotr said. they both laughed. "So, do you want to go grab something to eat?"

"Sure, what do you think about Lake Balaton?"

"Let's go!" Piotr decided.

Lake Balaton was a typical restaurant with the Społem label. They served Hungarian and Polish cuisine. In the good days, it used to provide service mostly to German coach trips. The interior design and numerous photos on the walls referred to Hungary and Lake Balaton. Maroon tablecloths, white napkins in silver holders completed the picture. The restaurant wasn't crowded, and the staff moved lazily as if they didn't even want to be there due to the late hour. Kamil and Piotr sat at the table in the far back of the room and began to look through the menu.

"What can I get you?" asked a waitress wearing a black apron and a bored facial expression.

"I'll have the stew and a beer, please," said Kamil.

"We're out of those."

"Well then, Hungarian Langos."

"We don't have that, either. We close in an hour. We only have cabbage rolls with meat."

"In that case, we'll have two of those and two beers," Piotr replied.

The waitress left taking the menus with her.

"I'm glad they have something at all," Kamil laughed. "So, if you don't mind me asking, how did you become a priest in the first place? I mean, after all, priests..." Kamil paused.

"I, what? I sin, here and there? Is that what you were going to say?" Piotr finished for Kamil, harshly.

"No, that's not what I meant. Don't get angry. I'm sorry," said Kamil, stuttering over every other word.

Piotr kept his gaze down and didn't speak. Then, his lips parted, and he said, in a hushed whisper, "You have no idea how long I have fought against this, running away into prayer or fasting, but after awhile, it would always come back stronger. For years, I've been stuck in this suspense, looking for a way out of these thoughts and desires. I even took psychoactive medicine for some time, in hope of getting rid of these annoying thoughts, but they didn't make me feel right. There was a time when I considered suicide, but I am a religious person after all. Now I live an illusion that the priesthood is my fate and my idea to live. I lie to myself that the only love I need in my life is the love I get from God."

Kamil had no idea what to say after hearing such a confession. He remained silent. Piotr paused for a while, but soon spoke again. "My mother died of breast cancer when I was eight. My parents were divorced, and I've never met my father. I was raised by my aunt, who was extremely religious. She wasn't perfect. She maintained drill and discipline at home, but it was still better than an orphanage. I loved her. She died two years ago. When I finished high school, I went to a theology course at the University of Lublin, mostly following her guidance. After that, I took all the priest vows and since then, I've been a pastor."

"Have you ever been with someone?" Kamil asked shyly.

"I had a girlfriend in high school, but in my last year I realized I was into guys. At university, I fancied one, but he didn't like me back and nothing happened. Apart from that, I have never met the right person." His gaze fixed on the plate and he moved the meat with a fork from one side to the other without eating it.

"Many of us have someone on the side, we just don't speak of it out loud. The church authorities tolerate it, as long as it doesn't have anything to do with pedophilia. After all, we are all just normal people, true-born humans, and we have a need of being close with someone. I know that one of the priests in the east coast unofficially lives with his boyfriend. I met him at the seminary. I think he knows about me, because we once spoke about it. I see him rarely, maybe twice or three times a year."

The waitress brought the cabbage rolls and opened two bottles of beer. Kamil and Piotr began eating. They were both famished due to the late hour and all that had happened at the cinema. Piotr devoured his dish like a lion that had just hunted its prey. Kamil watched his friend closely and, for a moment, he really wished he could cook something for him one day.

He never liked to cook for himself those sophisticated dishes he had learned from his mother. He was very good at preparing meats, especially roast beef with plums with the addition of numerous herbs. It was one of the main dishes prepared at their home, every Christmas or family celebration. Kamil imagined himself cooking such a roast for Piotr, the two of them in an apartment perhaps living with one another. Now that was a thought.

"And you. Are you a hermit?" Piotr asked abruptly with a slight grin on his face.

"Me?" Kamil felt confused. "Actually, yes." He laughed. "I also had a girlfriend in high school, but we only had sex twice. Later, I dated one girl from my hometown for three years, but it didn't work. We had sex now and then, but I don't think I loved her. I simply had a girlfriend, because everybody did, and you just had to have one. For over two years now I've been single. I have never paid attention to men before I saw you in the corridor." Kamil blushed surprised with his sudden honesty. "My teammates have always been simple and vulgar, so I've never thought about any of them in such way."

"Have you never been to TO-TU? Apparently, it's an unofficial pub for dating."

"Yeah, I heard of this place, but I've never even considered going there."

"Excuse me, we are closing in 20 minutes," the waitress snuck up on them and interrupted.

Piotr shook his head annoyed. "Fine, I'll have the bill, please."

After having paid the right amount and sipping down the rest of their beers, they slipped on their coats, taking their sweet time. They didn't feel like ending such a nice evening and having to step outside.

"So, how about you come over to mine for some tea?" Kamil asked bravely, not wanting the date to end so abruptly.

"Thank you for inviting me." Piotr frowned and rubbed the tip of his nose twice with his hand. Looking at Kamil with embarrassment, he said with confidence in his voice, "but I don't think it's such a good idea. It's only our first date after all," he added.

Kamil looked like a scolded pooch and lowered his head. He put his hands in his jacket pocket, spat carelessly into the snow, and, acting as if nothing had ever happened, responded, "Well, I suppose you're right…" Said Kamil.

"I have one more thing to tell you," Piotr carried on, frowning. His face grew gloomy and concerned. Turning his head to the side and pretending to wipe his nose with a handkerchief, he tried to tell Kamil what he wanted in the least painful and drastic way possible. As if nothing had ever happened. "Tomorrow, I'm leaving on a missionary seminar at Jelenia Góra for two months, where we will be kept in complete isolation."

Kamil could not believe what he just heard. He felt defeated, *You have only just met me today and you're already leaving me?* he wanted to scream at the top of his lungs.

Piotr understood everything from looking into his eyes. "I'm sorry, I didn't think today would go like this, and after the movie I didn't know how to tell you."

"OK. I understand," Kamil lied as he fought back

tears. He suddenly became aware of the cold around him, the chill of the snow nipping at his neck.

"Kamil, don't be angry, there's is nothing I can do to reschedule this. Give me your address and I promise to drop you a line." Feeling guilty, Piotr moved closer to Kamil. He grabbed his hand and gently stroked the back of Kamil's hand as he looked him deep in the eye. His voice, though hushed, seemed very sincere and tender. Kamil realized that in any other situation he would have instinctively pulled his hand out of Piotr's grip, but now he felt differently about everything.

Piotr took out a little notebook and wrote *Kamil Adamski, 19/21 Potulicka Street, 70-740 Szczecin.*

"Note my number, too, you can call. It's 556-12, area code 091."

"I can't promise I'll call, because I don't know if I will have access to a phone, but I will surely write."

"OK. I'll walk you home," replied Kamil.

"No, let me walk you. It would be better if nobody from the parish saw me in the middle of the night with a strange man."

They walked silently to Kamil's.

"It's that block of flats," Kamil pointed to it with his index finger stopping at a dark gate of an old building.

"Well, thank you for this lovely night," said Piotr stretching his arm out towards Kamil.

"No. Thank *yo*u," said Kamil, shaking Piotr's hand, looking him straight in the eye.

Kamil couldn't resist and pulled Piotr after himself into the old gateway. They both jumped at each other again, biting into each other's lips. Kamil pushed his whole body against Piotr's, pinning him tightly to a wall. Mad, intense snogging lasted over five minutes. They would pull away for a moment to gasp for some air, only to suck each other's lips again like hungry leeches. They acted passionately, grabbing each other's heads and pulling hair. Kamil quickly realized that he was about to cum yet again, this same evening. Suddenly, someone opened the door on the first floor and switched on the staircase lights. They broke free of each other and quickly stepped outside. They said goodbye to each other again, and Piotr reassured Kamil, with a lot of affection, that he will soon write him a letter.

Kamil, still stunned after what had just happened, returned home in completely soaked knickers.

Unable to fall asleep, he began to analyze, in detail, each scene he had experienced with Piotr. The very moment their knees touched at the beginning had aroused him tremendously. The gentle yet firm pressure and rubbing of the knees, which he now recalled, gave him goosebumps all over his body and sent shivers down his spine. He could describe the moment his hand unwittingly fell on Piotr's hand like it would in a six-volume book as the most erotic scene ever written. Holding hands in a firm grip, he felt that they were Siamese brothers who share the same blood. Kissing greedily Piotr's strong and masculine hands in his mind made him feel like a submissive boy ready to serve his master at the latter's will. That excited him even more, bringing his strong, warm erection to a near boil. Again, sucking on Piotr's lips in his thoughts, he felt the taste of his saliva and the smell of his body. He was like a vampire who wanted to drain all the blood from his victim and then devour him whole. Recalling all these stages and the slow rise of tension made his swollen penis explode, and all that with just one stroke. Now he was in heaven, it was an absolute earthquake for his body and soul.

11TH FEBRUARY 1986

Even though it had been over two weeks since his meeting with Piotr, Kamil was still dizzy as if coming down from a bad high. He couldn't find his way around. At work, Robert quickly realized that Kamil was unnaturally ratty and unable to focus on anything.

"Dude, what's up? Are you OK? he asked. "How about you take some time off?" he offered.

"I'm fine," Kamil grunted. "I'm just overworked."

He was already tired and completely cranky from checking his mailbox three times a day and constantly listening for his phone to ring. The record by Urszula called *Malinowy Król* was worn from being constantly played, and the adapter was red hot every night. Previously, he used to change the needle in the adapter every three months, now, he's done it three times over the past two days. The record was the only thing that reminded him of the man, without whom he could no longer imagine his future. Sometimes he would get so wound up that he imagined possible scenarios of Piotr's phone calls,

I will keep totally cool and indifferent, as if nothing had happened between us, Kamil lied to himself. *What an arse, how could he just leave me like this?* he thought.

Ever since he met up with Piotr, he quit his volleyball practice telling his teammates that he had an arm injury. He would never forgive himself if Piotr called during his absence. Before going to bed he would have five or six beers or half a bottle of wine.

At last, on the 11th of February, while Kamil was watching the evening news, someone loudly knocked on his door.

"Who is it?" asked Kamil. There was only one thought in his head, that it must be a message from Piotr. He opened the door so violently that he frightened the postman.

"I have a registered letter to Mr. Adamski."

Kamil literally ripped the letter out of the postman's hands, quickly signed the receipt and handed him a 20-zloty coin.

His hands were sweaty and shaking when he opened the letter. Finally, he began to read:

Dear Kamil,

First of all, I would like to apologize for not calling you for so long. Unfortunately, we only have one phone here at the main reception, which I have no access to. There is one phone booth in the village nearby, but the machine has been broken for the past three months.

Every morning I get up at six and we pray until nine, then we have breakfast and the prayer vigil lasts until dinner, meaning that we mainly read the Holy Bible. After dinner, we manage maintenance works on the priory grounds and trust me, there is something to do every day. Then we have an early supper, evening mass and I go to bed. We are not allowed to watch TV and we are only allowed to listen to the radio on Sundays. I just keep humming the soundtrack from the movie daydreaming about you. There's 20 of us here. Priests from all over Poland, each from a different parish.

Don't worry, I only have enough place in my heart for one Kamil King [pl. Król]. And he is the only one I think about when I fall asleep and wake up. When falling asleep, I recall every minute of our last meeting, which helps me live through these times of separation. Every single day I wonder about what you're doing at work, what have you been eating, what you're wearing and if you still smell of Wiarus, at least a little bit. I keep thinking whether you too sometimes think about me and miss me?

I have a weekend off in the beginning of the month, on the 1st and 2nd of March. I thought you could visit me, if you would like to? We could spend these two days together, rent some place in Szklarska Poręba or Karpacz, because it's close, and stay somewhere far away from the rest of the world.

Let me know if you would like to come visit me and if this date suits you? Last but not least, my Kamil Król, I'm sending you my favorite poem by Kofta:

Co to jest miłość

Co to jest miłość
Nie wiem
Ale to miłe
Że chcę go mieć
Dla siebie
Na nie wiem
Ile

Gdzie mieszka miłość
Nie wiem
Może w uśmiechu
Czasem ją słychać
W śpiewie
A czasem
W echu

Co to jest miłość
Powiedz
Albo nic nie mów
Ja chcę cię mieć
Przy sobie
I nie wiem
Czemu

[English translation]
What is love

What is love
I do not know
But it's nice
That I want him
All to myself
For how long
I do not know

Where is love
I do not know
Maybe in the smile
I can sometimes hear it
In the songs
And sometimes
In the echo

Pawel Kurczab

What is love
Let me know
Or say nothing
I want you
With me
And I don't know
Why

Yours forever,
Piotr

PS

Piotr Graczyk
Klasztor Benedyktynów [Benedictine Prior]
Kopaniec 38
58—512
Zielona Góra Voivodeship

As Kamil read the letter, the tears rose to his eyes. He was angry with himself to have judged Piotr so quickly. After having read the letter, at once all his strength and joy of life came back. The letter from Piotr seemed to be the most precious gift he has ever received. Even if he was to see Piotr for an hour, he would be happy to travel to the end of the world, no matter how long and tough the journey would be. Without wasting another second, he quickly sat down and began to write:

Dear Piotr,

You have no idea how happy you have made me by writing this letter. I have been so worried about you and I was afraid you might never want to see me again because I rushed things too soon. And that you wouldn't want to see me because I wanted everything to happen faster than it was supposed to. I understand that maybe you need more time.

Now, yet again, I believe that life is worth living! After we've parted I felt like a flower without water, which is destined to die, or a dog in a kennel, who has lost its owner and has no one to love. The days without you are dull and pointless. Each of them is bland and the same as every other. I, too, remember every detail of our first meeting and every word you've said. Every day I savor every minute I have spent with you, dividing it into seconds, just to live through it again. I am impatiently counting the days to the 28th February when I will next see you.

Only yours,
Kamil King
PS
I'll send you a telegram two days before my arrival to let you know what time I'll be coming.

28TH FEBRUARY 1986

The train to Jelenia Góra slowly rolled down the tracks. Even though it's been seven hours since Kamil set off, he didn't feel tired. The thought of seeing Piotr was like having jolts of energy burst through his body. He couldn't calm down, even if he wanted.

How can people travel to Paris or Rome by train, it would take like a week to get there, he wondered.

Sitting in a compartment, in a second-class wagon on a torn down seat covered in brown upholstering, the air was filled with the familiar, pervasive smell of cheap cigarettes and booze. That smell was everywhere--on trains, at train stations, in waiting rooms, restaurants and bars. He thought it really was the smell of his country.

Kamil stared through the window, passing numerous villages, towns and countless fields. Every so often, he would design new scenarios of the next two days. What will he do when he sees Piotr after such a long time? Should he pretend to be indifferent not to scare him away? Or should Kamil throw himself at him and kiss him all over, just like he wants to?

After waiting another hour for the last PKS coach to Szklarska Poręba, he finally felt relieved and excited to see his loved one soon. There were only four people travelling on his coach. It was already completely dark outside as the bus drove through a narrow serpentine road through the high mountains. The great dark black forest seemed as deep as hell. It immediately made him think of a childhood tale in which naughty children were sent to the forest from which they never returned. Long dark trees, each as tall as a factory chimney, stood closely next to each other and from a distance resembled thin giant men who could devour anything that moved. The hazy moon in the sky looked like a November night in one of those spooky and corny vampire movies where they're planning to overrun an entire village.

God, I think I'm travelling to the end of the world. Is this even the correct coach? Will I even get to see Piotr today?

Soon after eight, the coach reached the main station in the town center. Kamil immediately spotted Piotr outside wearing the same polyamide coat and skiing hat he had seen him in the first time they met.

"I can't believe you're finally here!" Piotr rejoiced, giving Kamil a little hug and patting his back, like men do. "I came here every hour, for every bus. I almost thought I wouldn't see you today." he chuckled.

"The train was over an hour late because of snow on the tracks, and then I barely managed to catch the last PKS bus. It must be fate, don't you think?" Kamil joked.

"Yes, it must be destiny. A lucky star has finally fated us to meet today." Piotr laughed, showing his perfectly straight teeth that were as white as snow. "I rented the cabin until Sunday night. There's a kitchen where we can prepare something to eat. I also bought a few things, so we can have a supper and wine," Piotr finished.

"Perfect for me," Kamil jumped up with joy and clapped his feet in the air. But because they were alone in a dark street, he accidentally brushed his shoulder against Piotr's body and smirked. It sounded like: I'm just getting started here, and you don't want to know what's going to happen next. He only thought about one thing, *He's Mr. Right, because he planned everything from A to Z the way I like, and that's why I love him.*

The room was in a big, old cottage at the top of a hill made out of wood with a concrete substructure in a mountainous style, known as the highlander building style (*styl górlaski*) adopted mainly for guesthouses based on Podhale folk art elements in the national culture such as furniture, household appliances, clothing, porcelain products, musical instruments, and souvenirs.

Although it was already dark, it looked like an oasis of peace in some deserted region. Kamil thought that this was exactly what he needed. The building had three floors with each floor featuring six rooms and two bathrooms. The interior was light and warm with a mixture of colors. Modern furniture was completed with chairs and wardrobes designed in a mountainous style. When they came inside, they smelled a pleasant floral scent, a citrus note with a touch of cinnamon. The whole bouquet screamed *sun* and *spring*, which were, unfortunately, still several months away.

There were two blue flowers placed on the windowsill in separate pots.

"They're hyacinths," said Piotr when he spotted Kamil staring at the flowers. "They smell good, don't they? I had to ask the owner what they were. If you want, you can take a shower and I'll prepare something to eat."

"That's a good idea, but what happened to a proper *hello?*" Kamil asked. Kamil looked at Piotr with such a hunger.

Piotr came closer, hugged Kamil and kissed him delicately. Kamil took the initiative and grabbed him, threw him onto the bed, and sucked his lips. This crazy kiss lasted a longer while. Finally, Kamil pulled away from Piotr and said, "Well, now I can go take a shower, and you. You get going with the supper. I'm starving." Confused Piotr laughed out loud, still laying on the bed.

In the shower, Kamil realized he was hard, again. He didn't care that things were moving too fast. He felt that he and Piotr were ready to break all rules, boundaries and limits that night. The erotic atmosphere, filled with sex in the air, hovered like a summer fog over the lake of pleasure.

"Food's served," Piotr said to Kamil as he entered the room. Kamil was wearing blue pajamas and his hair was still slightly damp. There were sandwiches with meat, paprykarz szczeciński and three kinds of canned fish. There were also two, big, fancy cups and a bottle of Egri Bikaver.

"Oh, how did you know I love paprykarz szczeciński?" Kamil asked, surprised.

"I didn't. This is the only thing I got at Supersam," Piotr laughed.

They finished their supper quickly along with the wine which fuddled their brains.

"Ok. I'm taking a shower and we're going to bed. You must be knackered," Piotr smiled towards Kamil.

Piotr disappeared with a towel hung over his shoulder.

Oh, I'll show you how tired I am, Kamil thought.

Piotr returned from the bathroom already wearing his pajamas.

"So, are we getting in?" asked Piotr.

"I suppose we could," Kamil pretended to be surprised with this proposal.

Piotr switched the lights off. Kamil snuck up on Piotr and pulled him into the bed. Kamil grabbed his hand and pulled him closer. They both got goose-bumps all over their bodies. Kamil took Piotr's pajama shirt in fistfuls and yanked at it till it slipped off from his body. Then, he wiggled his fingers around the hem of his pajamas and tugged at them till Piotr sat in nothing but his underwear. He grabbed Piotr's huge, pulsating penis ending with a very red head and pushed it deep into his throat. He began to suck it as voraciously as a starving newborn sucks its mother's breast. After a moment, Kamil's penis was also fully covered by Piotr's lips. The smell of Piotr's fresh, male body was mesmerizing. Kamil caressed every inch of his member with the tip of his tongue, again and again swallowing it all the way down his throat. He smelled and licked those beautiful, robust testicles resembling two, mellow kiwis.

The craze of two, hot bodies didn't last long. After a minute of caressing his lips by Piotr, Kamil's penis was already as tight as the hunter's bow ready to shoot at wild game. Kamil roared like a lion, curling up in a crazy outburst of pleasure. Piotr's throat was flooded with white, pearl liquid. After another two strokes of lips on Piotr's penis, Kamil felt something pulsating and a sudden, massive cum shot right into the middle of his throat. He hungrily swallowed every drop of his manhood, as if the liquid was a life-giving nectar that he didn't want to waste even the smallest drop of.

Afterwards, they just lay down on their backs, gasping madly for air and staring into each other's eyes in the shine of moonlight. After a while, they cuddled up and lay beside each other for a while and said nothing. Piotr's legs were completely interwoven with Kamil's. Piotr wrapped one hand around Kamil's neck and put his face on Kamil's chest, enjoying the scent of his skin. Kamil played in Piotr's hair from time to time, gently kissing and biting his left ear.

Kamil studied every inch of his friend's body. He loved his scent. It was amazing, the only one of its kind. He could savor the smell of his testicles for hours, his freshly washed hair and male feet. He loved his big, manly hands with visible veins, a flat, hairy stomach, which showed every muscle and hard butt cheeks covered with thick moss, which he could kiss and caress forever.

After an hour, the lips of the two lovers met again. Their tongues began to play a little erotic game, fighting and surrendering to one another. Piotr gently grabbed Kamil's penis. The steady movements of his hand, coupled with passionate kisses, quickly made Kamil hard. Wanting to return the favor, Kamil started licking and gently sucking the tip of Piotr's cock. It tasted like the most valuable specimen of a delicious exotic fruit that he was about to eat but at the same time he wanted to cherish for as long as possible to engrave its look and taste in his memory.

When this sensual dance of their bodies seemed to be reaching its climax, Kamil fiercely pushed Piotr onto his stomach. He began to delicately caress his hole with his tongue and lightly bit and pinched his hard buttocks. Piotr moaned with pleasure, whispering words now and then.

When Piotr's backside was moist enough, Kamil

used his liquid to enter his hole with one, swift move, pushing Piotr's whole body into the bed. Their hands locked in a wild hold, and Kamil instinctively slide into Piotr harder and harder, trying to push deeper and deeper into him as much as possible.

"Does it hurt?"'Kamil asked.

"No! It's great!" Piotr stuttered.

Kamil pressed his body to Piotr's even harder and began to bite on his ear delicately. Piotr moaned with pleasure, giving in fully.

"You're mine," he whispered, thrusting into Piotr as hard and as deep as he could go.

"You know that, Kamil, my dear," Piotr replied, crying in ecstasy.

At one point, Piotr opened his thighs a bit and pushed his buttocks out and up.

"Deeper!" he screamed.

Kamil couldn't resist anymore and exploded with a warm liquid right inside his lover's body, flooding him all the way to the top with his cum. Thousands of small needles pricked through Piotr's body, shaking him up like a cocktail mixer.

Kamil clung tightly onto Piotr. For a while longer, they lay like this, locked together into one, snogging and gasping for air. At around six in the morning, they finally fell asleep, satisfied for the first time in their lives.

1ST MARCH 1986

It was almost half past 12. Kamil opened his left eye a little.

"How's my warrior?" Piotr asked tenderly, passionately kissing his friend on the lips.

"Breakfast is ready," he chirruped happily. "What are the plans for today?" he asked.

"The plan is that we're staying in bed all day with you sitting on me," Kamil laughed.

"How about we walk up to Szklarka?" Piotr was persistent.

Kamil looked out the window; it was sunny and the white snow covering everything tempted him to go for a walk.

"I think Szklarka is a good idea," said Kamil.

Piotr went for a shower. Kamil unwittingly turned on the radio. After having listened to the news, he was happy to hear Madonna:

'...I was beat
Incomplete
I'd been had
I was sad and blue
But you made me feel
Yeah you made me feel

Pawel Kurczab

> *Shiny and new*
> *Like a virgin...'*

He loved this song. He didn't know English, but he had seen a translation of the lyrics in some newspaper and he remembered them very well. Just like that. When writing this song, did Madonna ever expect that somewhere, on the other side of the planet, in some communist country, there will be two men, who had just spent the night together, feeling exactly what she did? *God, this woman is an absolute genius!* Kamil thought.

After breakfast and a quick, but very intense dessert in the form of oral sex, they went outside.

There weren't many people in the streets. They passed by a greengrocers and stepped into a forest. When they realized there was nobody on the trail, they quickly grabbed each other's hands. Kamil looked around as if he had been there before and remembered something. He found the road, the trees and the whole scenery very familiar.

"Have you ever been here before?" Piotr asked.

"Yes, a long time ago, at a camp. I remember the waterfall was huge and scary," Kamil giggled. As they walked along the bushes by the side of the road, two little red deer suddenly jumped out and, crossing their path, bolted into the nearby bushes. It didn't last more than a few seconds.

"I'm not sure if those were does or bucks," said Kamil.

"Or maybe they were two lonely deer lovers who decided to escape from that forest for search of a better life," laughed Piotr. "Have you heard that animals can also be homosexual?" He asked, changing the subject.

"Yeah, I once read that a lot of grey swans of the same sex pair up and if something bad happens to one, the other dies of longing."

"How beautiful," Kamil became lost in his thoughts. Animals are more natural and vulnerable than us, and therefore more easily hurt. They don't act or pretend to be something that they're not. Seems so much easier, doesn't it?" Kamil shouted it out without even realizing it.

Piotr nodded and smiled and said, "that is beautiful, isn't it?"

They went on walking in silence for some time, only squeezing each other's hand from time to time. They both realized how fragile and new their relationship was when faced with the reality. The two happy last days that they had spent together somewhere at the end of the world seemed like a fabulous dream that must end sooner or later. They were not yet ready to go back to Szczecin, to work and live their normal life. The life where everyone is the same and relationships between two men are considered a perversion or illness. Given their line of work, they weren't even able to live together, let alone have a happy life together and share the ups and downs of everyday life like a normal family. They wanted to stay here forever. To live, in hiding or on another planet, or far away from everything in some distant northern land. Then they could finally truly be with each other, forever.

"I have recently read an article in *Polityka* about gay people in Poland. I was really surprised that they had published it," Piotr began, breaking the silence. "It's awful that we still have to live in hiding and we cannot even form societies. In countries like Holland or England there are a number of organizations, which

95

fight for our rights to live normally, without the fear of tomorrow. I'm not even going to mention America." Piotr didn't hide his indignation. His face was grim looking down. He kicked over a pebble lying in his way.

"I don't know if America is really that great," shyly suggested Kamil. "Don't you remember what Reagan said about the homosexual plague and that we're to blame when the first cases of AIDS came out?"

"Yes, you're right," answered Piotr. "But people probably need time. Some 30 years from now, I'm sure the American president will support gays and lesbians, and there will be a vaccine for AIDS, too, while here, in our Catholic country, chances are little will change."

"Do you think it will ever be possible for us to live together, hold hands and not be ashamed of our love?" Kamil asked sadly as if speaking of something completely unimaginable.

"I don't know, but what I do know is that something has to be done. We have to at least set up some association for the people to finally see that we exist. This country and its politics are not normal. It promotes losers faithful to their party, and locks up intelligent people, who have a brain of their own. What's with all these interrogations? Would something like this ever take place in a normal country?" Piotr was clearly irate. His face scrunched up in disgust. He paused for a moment, clearly waiting for Kamil to say something.

But Kamil couldn't say anything, now. How could he? He *is* one of the losers faithful to their party, a blind follower trying to better his life at the expense of others. Or maybe now he was no longer. Maybe things have changed?

"Say something!" Piotr spat. Kamil just stared at the ground. "After all, you too felt debased just because you're like this and you do not fit with the rest."

Piotr was clearly annoyed. His forehead was all wrinkled and his eyes were furious with hatred. He looked like a raging bull ready to attack upon seeing a red cloth. He stared at him, his eyes heavy as a rock, which overwhelmed Kamil for a moment. He stood there, charged like a storm and at the same time unexplainably powerless. Suddenly, Piotr took a stick lying on the road and threw it hard at a nearby tree. The stick bounced off the tree with great force, breaking into two pieces that flew into nearby bushes. Kamil couldn't move after seeing such a calm, free spirit lash out in anger for the first time. They didn't exchange a single word. Only in the distance could one hear the birds sing and the sounds of the forest.

Piotr gently took Kamil's hand and said, "I'm sorry for my behavior. I know it's not your fault." Kamil saw tears in his eyes.

They kept on walking on.

The waterfall looked exactly how Kamil remembered from a few years ago. A stream of water falling from a height crashed against the rocks, causing a little drizzle. White icicles hung on both sides of it resembling an ice castle from some distant, fairy land. It was beautiful. When they began snogging at the waterfall, they felt like invisible lovers at the end of the world. They returned holding hands, without speaking a single word, feasting on the omnipresent silence and their intimacy.

When they walked into town, they stepped into the only restaurant that was open at this hour. After returning home, they went straight to bed. Snuggled into one another. They stroked each other's backs and stared at the two hyacinths that stood on the windowsill.

They tried to savor every moment together, as they were aware of the fact that this was their last night together.

That night they made passionate love, without boundaries; like two Roman warriors who had to make love in hiding to avoid punishment. Now they could finally get the full taste of each other's perfect bodies. For those few hours, they became one.

Afterwards, they fell asleep in the early morning cuddling.

2ND MARCH 1986

Kamil woke up first. It was almost 2:00 p.m. For a moment, he stared at Piotr, examining every feature of his face and every detail of his body. He wanted to stop time, so that this room and this moment could last forever. Only now did he understand why people talk so much about sex. Sex with Beata was mechanical, stripped of any feelings. It was just another physiological act, just like defecating or urinating. Just something that he had to do. Now, when he had his first time with a man, everything went surprisingly naturally, without any unnecessary words, just their two bodies, insanely thirsty for each other's physical and emotional love. Sex with Piotr felt like a journey to an unknown planet, unknown, strange, and scary, but thrilling and exciting. He felt like someone who, for half of his life, had been looking at the world in black and white, and now, he has finally been given a kaleidoscope to look through, showing him endless possibilities where he could stop, admire, and truly feel.

Kamil slowly began to realize that being with Piotr was not only about sex, though. When he was with Piotr, he felt like a completely different person. Maybe a better, more special person than he usually was. He finally felt like he could accept himself for the way he really was. He felt that, with Piotr, he didn't have to act or pretend. He could finally be with someone and not worry about what that person will think of him. It may be that, for the first time in his life, he felt unconditionally loved. He realized that people didn't really fall in love with the person's sex, but with the right person, regardless of sex.

Suddenly it struck him that Piotr didn't really know anything about him. The biggest problem was Kamil's work and its nature. *God, if only Piotr found out where I work and that I was involved in the action, he would probably leave me right away.* What to do, and how to tell him? He felt that, because of Piotr, he was changing profoundly as a person.

* * *

Piotr's thoughts revolved around one thing and one thing only. He simply felt this guy just might be somebody important in his life. He finally felt happy, and most of that happiness might have to do with the fact that he could finally love someone. His life finally made sense. What he felt then was not the same as his platonic affairs in high school. Neither his brief and accidental physical encounters at the seminar for his work, whose sole purpose was to relieve sexual tension, were nothing compared to what he felt and experienced at that moment. He felt a special bond with someone who was like him, with a mature person with whom he was probably ready to spend the rest of his life. He was also aware that, for the first time in his life, he felt physically and mentally satisfied by the same person. However, when he thought about the near future, it seemed to him like a dead end. As a priest, he would have to flip his entire life upside down.

Suddenly, Kamil realized that his return train to Szczecin was leaving at eight in the evening and he will have to say goodbye to his loved one. Kamil began to sob and sniffle, which woke up Piotr.

"What's going on, teddy bear?" asked Piotr.

"I'm fine," responded Kamil in a moody and winey voice. "I must hurry up a bit because my train leaves at eight." Kamil went to the window and ran his fingers through the petals of one of the hyacinths.

He knew they would part soon, but he wasn't sure if Piotr felt the same way he did. Piotr approached Kamil to give him a hug, but Kamil stepped aside to avoid it. Piotr looked rather surprised.

"Wait, I'll make you breakfast," Piotr said. It seemed he didn't want to give up.

Kamil, pretending to pack his bag, passed by Piotr and rubbed his body against Piotr's, as if by accident. Piotr immediately got the message. He hugged Kamil tightly and tenderly. Kamil gripped Piotr firmly, with his hands on his hips, while his head was in Piotr's arms. In a sad and reproachful voice, he said, "I just realized that these are our last hours together," Kamil answered. "When will I next see you?"

"I'll be back in mid-March, so it's less than a month away. Will you manage? Can you wait?"

"You must not be aware of how powerful the strength of hope is. Of course, I'll wait. I will be your white mouse that learns how to swim," Kamil said, booping Piotr on the nose playfully.

'What does that mean?' Piotr asked, raising his eyebrows.

"Haven't you heard of that experiment with the mice and a fish tank?" Kamil asked playfully.

"No," said Piotr, confused.

"Well, once, in America, there was an experiment where a white mouse was put into a tank of water. The mouse only managed to swim for 20 minutes until it drowned. When the next mouse was put in it swam for 20 minutes like the last mouse. Only this time, they gave the mouse a ladder, which it used to get out. A day after that, the same mouse was put in the tank, but it was not given a ladder after 20 minutes. How long do you think it managed to survive, swimming?"

Piotr, sitting on the couch, was clearly absorbed and carefully listened to the story. Lying face down, he backed up his chin with his two hands and lifted his legs up.

"I don't know," he said quizzically. "Thirty minutes, maybe?"

"Nope. it swam for the next 40 hours because it believed that someone would finally pass it a ladder."

"I've never heard this before, but the story definitely makes an impression," Piotr said respectfully.

Kamil saw Piotr's black top hung on a chair.

"Can I have it? I want something of yours," he whispered. "It could be my little ladder to get me through the tough times."

He grabbed the T-shirt and gave it a hug.

"Oh my! It smells of you so much. What is it?"

"It's Alain Delon. I got these colognes a while ago for my birthday, and I've kept them to this day. You can keep that top… so long as I get something from you," Piotr said with a smile.

Kamil turned the radio on and they cuddled for a minute. It was Kora on the radio:

Mam w domu szafę bardzo starą
Z podwójnym dnem, z lustrami dwoma,
Gdy zaczną strzelać za oknami,
Będziemy w szafie żyć...

[Eng. I have a wardrobe at home, an old one
With a false floor, with two mirrors,
If they start to shoot outside,
We will live inside it...]

Lying on the bed with Piotr he realized that he had never been this happy before. They lay naked with their heads on opposite sides of the bed. Kamil gently began to massage Piotr's right foot by pressing and stretching its most sensitive areas. He once read an article in a newspaper that, in the old days, Japanese geishas were so well versed in massaging male body parts that they could make their clients addicted to them, after which the men only wanted to use the services of that particular geisha. For a moment, he imagined being such a *geisha* for Piotr. Piotr's feet were broad and masculine. Gently rubbing his toes, he slowly caressed Piotr's foot with his tongue and bit it lightly. After a while he did the same with the other foot. Piotr just lay there, purring like a happy tiger being scratched behind the ear. At the same time, he was impressed with his lover's erotic inventiveness.

* * *

When they got onto the PKS bus, they went to sit at the far back, so that nobody would disturb them. It was already dark outside, which meant they were safe for some cuddling. Sitting there, they cuddled and kissed hungrily, like tragic lovers who would never see each other again.

When they finally reached Jelenia Góra, Piotr accompanied Kamil to the platform. It was dark and cold on Platform 3. A thick snow began to snow sideways. Although there were four lanterns on the platform, only two worked, as the other two were broken. Apart from four old wooden benches and a broken neon sign with the words "Jelenia Góra" lit up, there was nothing else lighting their path.

A group of people waiting for the train in the cold gathered at one end of the platform under the working lamps. Piotr and Kamil both stood on the other end in the dimmest corner. Looking at each other, they both had anger in their eyes. Pretending to exchange nothing but a friendly handshake, they moved so close to one another that they appeared as one silhouette from afar. In spite of the cold, their clasped hands were wet with excitement. Kamil hugged Piotr, patting him even more strongly on the back. In what seemed like a friendly fashion, he touched Kamil's ear lightly with his lips and kissed it. A man passing by looked at them suspiciously, but they didn't care. They were in love.

Finally, they moved apart as the train pulled up next to the platform. Kamil got on the train. They stared at each other through the window for a moment. When the train started departing, Piotr waved to Kamil from the platform and blew him a kiss. Kamil returned the gesture.

* * *

On his way back to Szczecin, Kamil kept on thinking about what Piotr had told him about the politics in their country and the future that awaits them should they choose to stay together. He tried to fall asleep, but he couldn't. There was just the reflection of a face of a man, looking back at him from a dark window he was staring into, who for his whole life only did things in his own interest and what others told him to do. As he looked at the reflection of himself, he felt as though his reflection was a complete stranger. In only two days he felt as though his whole world was flipped upside down, and for the better.

He realized that he had never really been alive before. Suddenly his whole life seemed pointless. The work, where he felt so needed and which he liked so much, turned out to be some sort of great deception and manipulation that he was being subjected to. Piotr kindled a spark in his mind that didn't want to go out and that was slowly transforming into a small flame. Anger and rage towards the whole communist party and system grew inside him—the system in which the individual, creativity and freedom of thought meant nothing and the masses of anonymous people without personality and future had to follow yet another five-year plan imposed by the Party. He couldn't imagine going back to work and to his life, where he was still pretending to be someone he was not. There was only one word in his head and his mind, and that was AWAKENING.

13TH APRIL 1986

*Banquet venue of Teatr Współczesny in Szczecin, a
dinner party to celebrate the 50th performance of
'Poszukiwany, poszukiwana'*

The hall was located on the last floor of the theatre. A tall
ceiling with domes and huge crystal chandeliers
completed the atmosphere of uniqueness of this theatre.
The walls were upholstered with navy fabric with
numerous photographs and posters of various plays stuck
to it. The floors were parquet with three, long tables
situated in the middle of the room covered with dark
green tablecloths. On them were white porcelain bowls
of herring soused in vinegar. Eggs mayonnaise were in
blue bowls. Sliced ham and sausage were spread on long
silver trays, and pickled cucumbers were in clay brown
pots. The vegetable egg salad lay on a plastic yellow tray
and was sprinkled with fresh chives. Freshly chopped
cucumbers and tomatoes were served on small red plastic
plates. In a large bowl of pink glass was a pile of apples
and pears. At the end of the table, by the glasses, there
were cakes. Orange-yellow cheesecake with raisins
evenly cut into rectangles on golden long trays and
brownie cake sprinkled with a large amount of coconut
flakes on top that made it look as if someone had dipped
it in fresh snow. Every detail was refined to perfection.

The colorful tables looked like a lavish Easter feast in the Polish countryside. Vodka, Soviet champagne and orangeade were placed on a separate table.

Director Paprocki tapped his glass with a teaspoon a few times and asked everyone for their attention. All conversations in the room faded, and, just like that, everything was silent.

"I would like to thank everyone who's come here today. Today, we have gathered to celebrate a splendid success for our theatre, which, thanks to our friend, is talked about everywhere. The play *Poszukiwany, poszukiwana* and an amazing job done by Mr. Fabisiak had filled our theatre to the fullest. Above that, we have been invited for theatrical confrontations in Krakow at the end of May, where *Poszukiwany, poszukiwana* will compete against 15 other plays. Let's enjoy ourselves and celebrate our success!"

A thunderous round of applause roared around the room.

"Congratulations, Mr. Fabisiak, 50 performances and all sold out! There are no tickets left for the next month," said Paprocki.

Guests gathered at the tables laid with food. Conversations, laughter and glass clinking could be heard all over the place. Paprocki struggled to get through to Fabisiak, especially that the latter was already swarmed by groupies giving him congratulations.

"Thank you, director, for your faith and the opportunity you have given me."

"Congratulations! You were amazing!" said Anna Bałacka, kissing him on the cheek.

In the play, she took the role of Fabisiak's wife, and privately was his best friend.

Paprocki skillfully joined the conversation. He produced from his jacket pocket a clipping from the latest Głos Szczeciński (Voice of Szczecin) daily with a review of the performance. Raising his voice and getting everyone's attention, he read out an extract of the review.

"Well, isn't it fantastic! The review in *Głos Szczeciński* speaks for itself: 'Zbigniew Fabisiak in *Man–Woman Wanted* fills the entire stage with his charisma. Towards the end of the performance, Marysia conquers the hearts of the audience and the standing ovations are indeed well deserved, read out the director.'"

"Bravo! Bravo! I've always believed in you," shouted excitedly Kasia, a cloakroom attendant and a close friend of Fabisiak.

Fabisiak was wearing a light pink shirt and black trousers. He was wandering around the guests, with bits of make-up still left on his face, bursting with pride. He thought of his mother for a moment, how proud of him she will be.

Fabisiak has never felt prouder. The years of humiliation and playing supporting roles were suddenly erased from his mind. The only thing that mattered was the present. He wrote a long letter to his mother, attaching to it all press clippings and photos from the performance. He knew that she always loved him and believed in him. Although he never officially talked to his mother about being gay, he felt that she knew and loved him the way he was. His father had been dead for several years, but Fabisiak never truly missed him. He never heard a good word from his father. Instead, he would always humiliate him and make fun of him, calling him 'mommy's daughter'. To this day, he remembered the words his father has said to him over and over again. "Look at yourself, you'll grow up to be a nobody, living off that acting thing like a loser." If only he could show him how well it had turned out for him and how everyone respects him now.

"Well, very good for an actor, who mainly plays supporting roles," Milewski, one of the actors, spoke.

Fabisiak truly hated him. Milewski was around 10 years younger and would get any role he wished. He was tall, manly, athletically built, handsome brunet with a small scar on his cheek. Reportedly, he had trained as a boxer when he was young. He was often egoistic, jerky and extremely vulgar. Unfortunately, despite all this, he was still liked by everyone a lot more than Fabisiak. "Well, someone has to play complex and ambitious roles because younger inexperienced actors would not cope well with them." Fabisiak answered back.

"Yes, it's true that not every real man could empathize with the role of a woman as well as you do." Milewski said, sending Fabisiak an angry bull's-eye.

"Yes, I agree with you," said Fabisiak in a calm and balanced voice, sneering like a poker player who was about to win the hand. "Real men like you are certainly the best in the role of gorillas in children's performances where they say nothing but just roar loudly and run around like bumbling idiots do."

All the guests burst out laughing. Fabisiak triumphed and he smiled in glee.

"Don't listen to him. You know what he's like," Anna gave him a hug. Fabisiak had been friends with Anna for years. She was the first person at the theater to talk to him on his first day of work. She was the most kind-hearted person so everyone at the theater was fond of. Her husband was an engineer and they had a five-year-old daughter named Magdalena. Anna and her husband often invited Fabisiak for holidays or family celebrations. She was a guardian and a confidant to him, a person with whom he could talk about his problems and love tribulations. They often acted on stage together, only Anna usually played the main roles.

The party was slowly coming to an end. Few people were left standing by the tables with food and alcohol. The rest formed several groups scattered around different parts of the room. Most people were already pretty drunk. There were loud conversations, shouting, laughter and even the sound of broken glass coming from either end of the room. Some shouted at others so that the music in the background was barely audible. Some had already started heading home. Some helped others stand because they were too drunk to make it to the door. One of the actresses got her blue dress caught up by the edge of the table. She fell on the floor, but luckily was unharmed. Two drunken men standing next to her tried to help her up. Unfortunately, one of them slipped on a piece of egg mayonnaise that had been dropped on the floor and he ended up falling on top of the woman. When the three of them finally got themselves up, they all couldn't stop laughing. For those standing on the side, the whole act looked like a scene from a Charlie Chaplin film, only without the cake.

"The booze is running dry, but the night is so young." Anna screamed at the top of her lungs. "It's my brother's birthday today. I invite you all over to his house for the rest of tonight, and we're going to have a hell of a time!" Then she let out a loud, excited scream

A few squiffy people were eager to go. Fabisiak,

Anna and a few other workers got dressed and left the building. They got into taxies and left for Anna's brother's house.

* * *

After returning from the mountains, Kamil was charged with so much positive energy that he sometimes had the urge to jump with joy on his way to work or at the office. That didn't escape the attention of his colleague, Robert who quickly noticed that Kamil became much more optimistic and talkative than usual as of late. When they chatted, Kamil was gesticulating a lot and was strangely excited, with his eyes laughing and glistening as if he were on some uppers. It wasn't until Robert asked for the second time, as if in passing, what Kamil did on the long weekend when he took last Friday off. A bulb then went off in Kamil's head. He realized his behavior must have changed and he needed to exercise more caution. Feigning indifference, he told Robert about the wonderful weekend he had spent with his mother and his old friends.

He got a raise at work and was tasked with the responsibility of a new region. A few times he even asked Robert if it was easy to leave their job, but Robert became suspicious and Kamil quickly ended the subject. He decided to leave it for another time.

When Piotr returned, they spent every waking moment together when they could. They'd cuddle and kiss and laugh all over. Sometimes in Kamil's flat, having sex to Madonna's and Urszula's songs, other times in random places in Szczecin. They enjoyed walking up to Bismarcka Towers, where they would spend hours staring into the landscapes of Szczecin. They also often visited an animal shelter bringing the shelters more rice, groats and food leftovers. In the future, they wanted to adopt a dog from a shelter. Kamil was brought up with stray dogs that his mother used to bring from the street and he always had the opportunity to name them. Kamil's father disapproved, but he saw how happy it made his wife, so he got used to it.

Kamil thought at least a few times how he could introduce Piotr to his mother. Having dinner at his mother's, he was bursting with energy and his mouth wouldn't stay closed for a second. When telling his mother about the training in the mountains, he snuck in the character of Piotr, his new friend, several times. He talked vividly about how beautiful the Szklarka waterfall was in winter and what a great time he'd had in the mountains and during the training itself. When talking about the camp, he was so overwhelmed and distracted that he mistakenly sweetened the same tea twice.

Listening to his story, his mother realized that the last time she'd seen Kamil so happy and cheerful was when he was very young and came back loaded with new experiences from a distant trip he had gone on with a group of good friends. Kamil still didn't know how to tell his mother that Piotr was a man that he loved and with whom he would like to live and spend the rest of his life.

Their innocent love was blooming, and their systematic meeting resembled a life of an unofficial couple, who planned on spending the rest of their lives together.

15TH APRIL 1986

When the alarm clock rang, Kamil switched it off with a quick swat. Piotr was still fast asleep, cuddled into Kamil. They didn't move for the next five minutes, absorbing each other's presence.

"Oi, they'll fire me, and my husband, the priest, will not be able to support me with just the money from the collections,' Kamil joked.

Piotr laughed out loud and only then did he get up.

"I'm half dead," said Piotr. "You were really exhausting…" he smiled to Kamil.

"From what I understand, you like this kind of exhaustion," replied Kamil with a sneaky grin on his face, before giving Piotr a strong slap on the butt.

Kamil took the bread out of the cabinet and put the milk on to heat. After getting cheddar cheese and a jar of strawberry jam from the fridge, breakfast was almost ready. He took the milk off the gas soon before it boiled over and poured it over two cups with cocoa powder in them. The smell of freshly made cocoa filled the kitchen. When they were having breakfast, a new song by Bajm came on.

"*Miałeś rację nigdy tak nie było dobrze jak teraz [Eng. You were right it has never been this good before]*" Beata sang.

"So, where to next?" Piotr asked, ready to plan out their next date. "Maybe Szmaragdowe?"

"Yeah, that's a good idea."

Saying goodbye to each other, they snogged at the door for a long while, until Piotr left first.

At work, Kamil was alone, as Robert had taken a few days off. He thought of his first night with Piotr, the night at the cinema where their lustful journey began, how they exchanged pleasantries for the first time. Kamil's cock stirred in his pants, pushing up against the denim in his jeans. He tried returning to the folders on his desk, but his mind wandered to the image of Piotr's body. Every so often he would peek at his watch, but the hours seemed to be taking forever. *Shit, how am I going to wait until our next meeting? Maybe I can come to the vicarage and pretend to be a client?* he laughed inside. *Piotr won't be happy, but I have to go and see him, at least for a moment.*

After leaving work, he went straight to Piotr's vicarage. When he got there, he saw the woman in the babushka, Ms. Maria, who was a homemaker. When she saw Kamil she spoke quickly and loudly. "The priest doesn't have time today. He's busy!"

"I know, but I only need a minute."

"I've already said, he does not see clients today!" she screamed.

Kamil was surprised, as he did not expect such a reaction from such a calm, elderly lady. Suddenly, the vicarage door opened and two men around 40 years of age stepped out. They were wearing the same black trench coats and had a very bleak look on their face. As they passed Kamil, they stepped out onto the street.

It seemed strange to Kamil. Taking advantage of

this opportunity, he jumped through the doors, and past the elderly lady.

The elderly lady walked in right after him, still shouting, "I told you! The priest doesn't see clients today!" She jumped in front of him with a speed he didn't expect her to have, an ugly frown drooped across her face. At the same time, the office door swung open. Piotr stepped out of the office; his face blushed over red. Kamil's heart leapt as their eyes met. He wanted to run across the church and bear hug Piotr, but he had to resist. Ms. Maria watched them intently. Kamil expected at least a kind hello, or perhaps a smile. But Piotr's eyebrows furrowed, his forehead wrinkled. Then, he shouted across the church right at Kamil, "I said I was busy! Wait outside!"

Confused, Kamil stepped outside, his vision blurring. *Was he talking to me?* Kamil thought. He wanted to believe he wasn't, but Piotr's eyes burned into Kamil as he yelled. After 10 minutes of waiting outside, another, bald man in his 50's left. *What is going on here?'* he thought, getting completely lost in the whole situation.

When Kamil went back inside, Piotr asked him in.

"I told you not to come here!" he said, trying to contain his anger to a hushed whisper.

"I'm sorry. I just wanted to see you," said Kamil, looking at Piotr with apologetic eyes and bowing his head down like a repentant puppy.

"What did you come here for?"

Kamil did not recognize him, this was not the Piotr he knew. This one was cold and up to the point. He looked at Kamil with such icy eyes that it made Kamil freeze

"Tell me, what's going on?" asked Kamil as he fought back tears.

"We were supposed to see each other at yours and in random places!" his eyes were full of hatred.

"I know!" Kamil raised his voice. "Tell me what this is about, or I'm not moving an inch!" he pushed.

"I can't tell you now." Piotr whispered. "Someone might be listening," Piotr didn't give up.

But Kamil didn't care for secrecy in this moment. He loved Kamil, and he thought Piotr loved him. He would not be spoken to like this by someone he loved. "No! Either you tell me now, or you will never see me again!"

Piotr paused for a moment, staring at his desk. He seemed to be collecting his thoughts.

"Fine," Piotr said, defeated. "Sit down."

Piotr came outside for a moment to speak to Maria. "Please, go to the kitchen and start preparing the evening meal," said Piotr in a hushed whisper as best he could. Maria slowly nodded and headed off to one of the side rooms of the church.

Kamil sat there muddle-headed, awaiting clarification. He felt like he had been slapped in the face but didn't know what for. The whole situation seemed bizarre, and Piotr's unusual behavior heralded a looming disaster.

Kamil sat down fuming with anger and waited for some explanation. Why was Piotr acting like this? Didn't he want a life where they could be themselves out in the open, together as lovers like anyone else would? Kamil tried to remain calm, tried not to yell or cry.

Making sure that all the doors were closed, and Maria had left, Piotr slowly began to speak. "What I'm about to tell you now has to stay between us," Piotr threatened him. "Telling you, I'm putting myself in grave danger, but I can see I won't win with you on this." He paused.

"I cooperate with the Komitet Obrony Robotników."

"I guess you know what that is?""

Kamil nodded.

"What we have here is a special machine on which we print leaflets. The leaflets will contain anti-government slogans informing the people about the lies of the communist regime. For more than three years I've been a secret collaborator of the KOR acting on behalf of the Church. On May 1st, during the great procession that will walk through the streets of Szczecin to celebrate the Labor Day, we'll want to distribute over 3,000 of these leaflets. This is part of a larger protest action being prepared by the Resistance in all major cities throughout Poland. I am responsible for the actions taking place here in Szczecin. Everything is ready, and the machine with leaflets is in my basement. Now you know everything.

Piotr lowered his eyes, waiting for a response. Kamil looked at Piotr with tears in his eyes. After hearing Piotr's words, Kamil froze in disbelief for a moment. His head nearly exploded from the amount of new information to absorb. It was all happening too fast for him. He realized it was the best time to let go of the burden that he had been carrying for so long. He knew that could end their relationship, but this might be the only time he'll have ever mustered up that much courage. He couldn't and didn't want to go on like that, without being completely honest with Piotr and his own conscience.

"I, too, have to tell you something. Since a few months ago, I've been working as an official in the SB. On the day I first met you at the corridor, I was put into an operation. I was to collect information, remember the surnames, nicknames and phone numbers"

Piotr raised his eyebrows high and looked very surprised. He stared at Kamil with his pupils well dilated. Slightly gaping, the cheeks of his face all collapsed. For a moment he looked as if he'd just seen a corpse.

"Oh, now I understand," said Piotr. "Since the beginning, something was off."

Kamil looked at Piotr in slight disbelief, making a silly face. He frowned and pouted his lips. His eyes narrowed to the size of a small coin.

"What are you talking about?"

"Back then, at the hearing, everybody was called into rooms number 3, 5, 6 and 7. Only you were called into number 4, which, to be exact, I never saw you leave. For some time now, I was planning to ask you about this."

Hot tears ran down Kamil's cheeks. He reached for Piotr's hand in a moment to find some comfort in his touch, but Piotr yanked it away.

"When were you going to tell me?" Piotr asked, coldly.

"I wanted to tell you when we were away in the mountains, but then I heard your views. I was too scared to lose you. On my way back, I kept on thinking about what you said, back then, about our politics and life here. Now I can see that I'm part of a twisted state regime that destroys its citizens' freedom and has nothing to do with democracy. I wanted to give up the job and find something new. Please, forgive me."

Kamil put his hand on Piotr's shoulder. A sinister silence followed for a long moment. Piotr felt as if he had received a blow on the head. On one hand, he knew that the news would throw Kamil off his feet, but he didn't expect receiving that strong of a feedback. Piotr's face was fire red.

Kamil's face, however, was all as dim and pale as a sheet of paper. Because the atmosphere in the room was unbearable, Kamil fidgeted, still in tears. He wanted to get out of there as soon as possible and never return. Piotr, taking a deep breath with all the strength he had left and defying common sense, gently put his hand on Kamil's shoulder.

"Don't cry. I just need some time," said Piotr, crying. Kamil couldn't believe what he had just heard. The man he met only recently now wants to quit everything and turn his life upside down because of him.

Stuttering incessantly, Kamil stammered: "You can't do it. I can. I've given it good thought, believe me. I'll explain everything later."

Piotr seemed to have never been more convinced of anything in his life than he was of those words. For the first time ever, he felt that he needed to rebuild and re-evaluate himself and his life. He finally realized that he certainly didn't want to be a priest! They stood there for a moment, embracing each other in silence. Kamil, cuddling his head into Piotr's neck, was intensely sniffing Piotr's body and sweat. If Kamil weren't drowning in his arms, he couldn't stand still on his feet because of everything that had just happened. His legs felt made out of cotton, and he could hardly keep his balance.

Kamil stood up, hugged Piotr and began kissing him passionately on the lips. Piotr only resisted for a moment, but soon gave in. They were both crying, kissing lovingly for a longer while.

"I love you," Kamil whispered.

"I love you too, you have no idea how much. I will be writing a letter to the Bishop informing him that I want to give up my priestly vows. I'm leaving the church."

"You can't do that!" Kamil yelped.

"I can. I've already thought this through. Trust me. I'll explain everything later."

They stood there, hugging, without speaking a single word.

"You need to go. Now!" Piotr stepped away, practically pushing Kamil over in the pew. "We can't stay here together for too long because they might begin to suspect something at the vicarage," Piotr said in a commanding tone, trying to get rid of Kamil.

He realized that Kamil had been here for too long a time, and he still needed to get in touch with people from the underground and settle some matters regarding the action planned for May 1. Piotr, as the main person responsible for the action, had to have the perfect alibi for that day. Officially, May 1, he was to be delegated to a parish in another city to celebrate an arranged fictional mass. This whole undertaking required the work of several people with whom he had to get in contact and determine the details.

"I have an idea," said Kamil joyfully. "I can take the machine and the leaflets to my place and look after them until the march."

"No! That's too dangerous!" Piotr protested.

"It would be a lot more dangerous if you kept it here. I have a little shed at my mum's plot. It will be the best spot, because no one will look for it there."

Piotr thought for a moment, scowling.

"Actually… you might be right," he admitted.

The machine in shape and appearance, looked like a cash register, but a bit smaller. It was all made of metal and covered in gray paint. It didn't look like any complex contraption at all. Inside, two metal walls supported two large metal crankshafts. Underneath was a small paint container. The machine was foldable into a brown 50 x 60 cm case which could easily be mistaken for a travel suitcase. Three, long rows of paper leaflets of a 10 x 10 cm size, printed with red paint were wrapped in foil. Kamil read the text:

'*RELEASE POLITICAL PRISONERS!!!*' and '*PROGRAM OF THE PARTY FOR THE PEOPLE: THROUGH PRICE RAISES TO FAMINE!!!*'

"Wait here, I'll get you a taxi, "said Piotr.

Kamil caught a glimpse of himself in the metal wall of the machine. He hardly recognized himself. Kamil repeatedly watched various films and read a number of historical books about people who made sudden decisions that would completely change their whole life overnight. He always thought that never happened in real life, and certainly not in his. After all, his life was orderly, planned and predictable in almost every inch. However, all that changed when he met Piotr. For a moment he wondered what would have happened if somebody else had been sent to that action or had he called in sick on that day. What would have happened to Piotr? Kamil couldn't recognize himself. He just realized that, within the space of a moment, he went from a Secret Service officer to a secret collaborator of the Resistance. Could it be destiny that his eyes met with Piotr's in the corridor on November 15?

Piotr came back after 10 minutes. "He's here already. Be careful. It will probably be wiser for us to meet somewhere in public every other time. That way we'll both be safer," said Piotr in a firm voice.

"I agree," replied Kamil eagerly. "Remember, if something happens, don't do anything stupid. Please," said Piotr. "This is not just about you and me anymore. Many more people than you think are involved. If something happens to me, someone will contact you sooner or later."

"I understand, I'll remember," said Kamil, squeezing Piotr's hand.

"I love you!" Kamil kissed Piotr deeply on the lips for the last time. "Goodbye," he whispered, hugging him.

Shortly after, Piotr took the suitcase and quickly left the church office, closing the door behind him. Kamil got into a taxi and drove off to his mother's house.

18TH APRIL 1986

Main Police Station, Mazurska Street in Szczecin,
Captain Cegielski's office.

Militia Headquarters, Mazurska St. Szczecin. Interrogation room where Lieutenant Cegielski interrogated Fabisiak on November 22, 1985. In the room, there were two large oak desks and four plain pine chairs painted in black. The old yellow curtains were completely drawn, making the room and its hazel walls seem brighter than they actually were.

Nothing has changed since Fabisiak's last interrogation. The same PVC tile was on the floor. There was a gray lamp and a black telephone on each desk. Cegielski, in his uniform, sat at his desk smoking a cigarette and skimming through the last page of *Głos Szczeciński* with a sports section. He sniffled as he massaged his forehead to alleviate the throbbing headache. Even though he had already taken two aspirins, they didn't seem to work. He must have been coming down with a cold.

It was four in the afternoon and Cegielski was just getting ready to leave.

"Sir, there's someone here to see you, "the lieutenant called.

"Tell them to come back tomorrow. I'm knackered."

123

"He insists it's urgent and he has to speak to you today, Sir."

"Fine, let him in."

Fabisiak entered the room. He was wearing a black cotton coat and gray trousers, coupled with black ankle boots with a small heel. At first, he looked a little insecure with his slight hunch. He was still running through his mind the first interrogation with Cegielski and his rude behavior after which he couldn't sleep for a few nights. Cegielski put down the newspaper and put out his cigarette making a very displeased face. His head was literally bursting with pain.

"May I,"' Fabisiak walked to the desk, cautiously.

"Yes, have a seat." Cegielski pointed at the chair. Fabisiak noticed that Cegielski was no longer the monster and sadist that he remembered from the last interrogation. It was clear from the dark circles under his eyes and the slightly sweaty forehead that he was sick and tired.

"Oh, it's you, Fabisiak, I was just leaving, so I hope it's something important. You have five minutes."

"I have information. Can I take a seat?"

Cegielski nodded and pointed to a chair. Then he leaned back in his chair slightly. After the last interrogation, Fabisiak wouldn't have been surprised if Cegielski were to slap him right in the face just for Fabisiak breathing the same air as him.

"I just wanted to report on what I've heard at my friend's name day party."

"To the point, Fabisiak. I don't have time." Cegielski raised his voice.

"Well, a few days ago, we held a banquet at the theatre due to our performance coming onto the stage for the 50th time."

"Oh, yes, Fabisiak, I've heard and read the reviews in a newspaper. Did you come here to inform me of that, or do you have something useful?" Cegielski commanded.

"Well, you know, sir, afterwards, one of my friends invited a few people to her brother's name day party. That brother of hers is also a member of our society, and a few of my older friends were there. I'd had a bit too much to drink and I needed to use the bathroom, because I felt sick. When I was vomiting, I accidentally overheard some conversation between two people in the bathroom. Some employee of the police, or some other cell, is in a very close relationship with a priest, who is involved in printing leaflets at the vicarage."

"Who says so?" Cegielski's head perked up.

"I don't know who, because when I came out there was nobody there anymore."

"Which parish? What's the name of the priest?" Cegielski bombarded Fabisiak with questions.

"They didn't say," Fabisiak knew he was explaining himself poorly.

"I really hope this isn't some drunk, gay bullshit." Cegielski raised his voice. "Write the name, surname and the address of the owner of this flat. We'll check it out. Anything else?"

"No, that would be all. If I know anything more, I'll let you know. Goodbye," said Fabisiak.

"Right," replied Cegielski, gathering his things to leave.

23RD APRIL 1986

Sticking to their earlier agreement to meet out in the wild every other time, Kamil was travelling to Szmaragdowe Lake. He liked the idea of changing venues for their dates every other time, because he always liked spending time outdoors. In spite of his joy, he knew it was for their safety, and to protect the bond that they shared. Kamil knew that if any of his colleagues ever found out about his relationship with Piotr, it could end very drastically for the two of them.

Riding on the bus towards the right-hand bank, he realized that he hadn't visited this place for a long time. *It was around five years ago, with my mother,* he remembered. When he got there, it was only 5:40.

The magic of this place has always put him in a romantic mood. Beautiful, clear, emerald water, with reflections of numerous beech trees and calcium sides, the birds singing and an old, little bridge from the beginning of the century created an atmosphere of uniqueness of this place. When he was there in the past, he always imagined coming there accompanied by the person he loved; that they would walk holding hands and looking each other in the eye. Often, seeing the couples who were coming there, he felt jealous and slightly bitter that he was usually alone. It made sense now, given who he loves. Now he was waiting for Piotr and intended to do with him all the things he had dreamt of before, hoping they would spend an unforgettable, romantic time together.

Piotr could not have thought of a better spot, Kamil thought.

* * *

It was already 6:05 p.m. and Piotr still wasn't there. Some passersby would walk by the lake for a moment and disappear among the trees. One couple went up the hill towards a bridge, to admire the view from up there. The sun slowly began to set and white clouds formed in the sky, reminding him of the cotton candy from his childhood days. Apparently, if the light is good on sunny days, one can see sunken wagons from the old chalk mine lying at the bottom of the lake. But it was too dark now. For a moment he stared at the fish that would swim up to the shore in search of food. Unfortunately, he had nothing that he could give them. He was sure that the fish were carps, because he remembered the lake had been artificially stocked several years ago. The evening wind gathered for a moment and blew some dry leaves on the water surface.

Kamil started getting a bit worried past 6:15 p.m. Piotr was never late.

Maybe something came up, or there was too much traffic, he thought. In the distance he saw the familiar couple who was already returning from up the hill and heading back to the city. It was getting dark and cold.

127

By 6:45 p.m., Kamil was legitimately concerned. To vent the tension, he started kicking a bench that stood by the lake. It was getting really chilly, so he rolled up the sleeves of his sweatshirt. Whenever he was tense or anxious, he would involuntarily bite his right cheek from the inside twice to feel the familiar taste of his own blood in his mouth.

At quarter to seven, he was already pretty scared and decided to go to his parish. They had agreed that he would never come there again, but he could feel that something was wrong.

Approaching the vicarage, a looming, evil silence hit him. When he knocked on the door, nobody answered. He knocked harder. He heard scraping on the other side. The door was finally opened by Ms. Maria, an elderly lady in a babushka.

"Is priest Piotr here?"

"He is not, and he won't be here for some time," she said harshly.

"What do you mean he's not here? Tell me, what happened?" Kamil raised his voice. "I've already told you, he won't be coming back for some time," she said emotionlessly, trying to get rid of Kamil.

"Tell me what happened? I'm begging you! I was supposed to see Piotr and he never showed up," he cried, feeling terrified. "I'm a good friend of his," he said, fighting back his tears and looking her straight in the eye. "Please tell me, what happened? I want to help him," he insisted.

She spoke dispassionately, clearly trying to get rid of Kamil. Her eyes expressed suffering, and her pale, wrinkled face showed enormous pain. Standing there helplessly, she lowered her head. Her arms sank so that she looked even smaller than she was. Fighting her own thoughts, she turned her back to Kamil and started adjusting her headscarf nervously. but as he was leaving, she said loudly in a shaky voice, "He was arrested!"

"What?" Kamil turned. His jaw nearly dropped to the floor. His heart thudded in his chest.

"Yes, they came this morning and took him. Later, they searched his room and the whole vicarage, but thankfully they found nothing. Straight away, me and a vicar called the bishop. He was here and left around two hours ago."

"Where did they take him?"

"From what the bishop managed to find out, he is held in the prison on Kaszubska Street. God knows how long they will keep him there."

"Thank you," said Kamil running out of the vicarage.

"I'll try to contact you when we know something," she said.

Leaving the parish he felt like he had been hit over the head. He seemed to know that something had happened, but all the time he didn't realize how serious the whole situation was. His legs carried him all over the street aimlessly. He was having all sorts of thoughts. Will Piotr make it there? Will he ever see him again? He realized that, in reality, there was nothing he could do to help him.

Returning home, he decided to pass by the Kaszubska prison. From behind the wall, he wanted to look at the window of the cells and fool himself that he could see Piotr's silhouette for a moment.

A few women and one man were standing near the wall, on the other side of the prison. Kamil stopped at a safe distance a few meters away and kept observing. Nothing happened for over 10 minutes. Exactly at eight, somebody from a cell on the second floor shouted: "Go!"

One of the women with gaudy make-up screamed, "To Ginger from 19C. I saw a lawyer, I'll write you a letter. I'm waiting!"

Kamil came significantly closer and watched her for a moment of jealously.

"You, your turn now!" she suddenly said to Kamil.

Kamil, surprised with the whole situation, couldn't say a word.

"Quickly now! Before the guards change," she hurried him.

"I have a message to a priest, but I'm not sure if he's there," he managed to say.

"Oy! Do you have a Crow there?" screamed the woman.

"He's here!" said the voice from the window.

"'Speak! But hurry!" she shouted.

Kamil gathered all his strength and screamed at the top of his voice.

"To Crow: Grey Swan will wait, and the white mouse will never drown!!!"

Tears flowed down his cheeks. There was dead silence for over five seconds.

"Done!" Finally someone from the cell window shouted.

Kamil was now crying without hiding it. The woman with make-up came up to him and gave him a light hug.

"They do come out, sooner or later," she said in a sad voice.

He still cried all the way home, and the people who passed him in the street gave him funny looks. But he didn't care, because he was in love and that was the bravest thing he could be in his life.

When he walked into his flat, he opened a bottle of wine and turned on the radio. He drank half a glass in one sip. It was Bajm playing on the radio:

Co mi, Panie, dasz w ten niepewny czas?
Jakie słowa ukołyszą moją duszę, moją przyszłość na tę resztę lat?…

[Eng. Oh, Lord, what will you give me in these uncertain days?
What words could rock my soul, my future for all the days to come?...]

He quickly turned off the radio, laid on the bed, cuddled Piotr's T-shirt and fell asleep.

24th APRIL 1986

Kamil's flat, Potulicka Street in Szczecin

He only slept a few hours with breaks, turning from side to side. Once flooded with sweat, he threw the quilt on the floor so that in a moment he would be all chilled and then he covered himself all the way up to his head again. Finally he woke up in the morning 15 minutes before the alarm clock. He felt that he had a high fever and terrible chills. After all that had happened the day before, he could not imagine going to work and pretending that everything was all right.

When he looked in the mirror he looked as if he'd been beaten to death. He gave a call to work without thinking, saying that he had a cold and that he would not be back until Monday. After all, he had all the symptoms of a cold, although he knew that it was caused by great stress. A terrible headache and bone pain made him unable to move out of bed.

After taking two aspirins, he lay in bed and stared blankly at the ceiling for an hour, waiting for the tablets to work. Thinking about the events of the previous day, he finally fell asleep tired of pain and fever. He woke up around one in the afternoon. The headache clearly eased off and he felt a little better now.

God, what will I do during these four days?

Without hesitating, he dialed his mother's number. Nobody answered for a moment.

"Hello, Adamska speaking," a familiar voice said.

"Mom it's me. Will you be home today?"

"Yes, what happened?" his mother asked.

"Nothing, I have two days of vacation left and I thought I'd visit you," he announced pretending to be confident.

"Come along, I don't have any plans. I will prepare a quick dinner and you can stay overnight if you want," she replied all overjoyed.

The day was dark and cloudy. The falling rain and gray sky gave away all the depression and mood of Kamil. He reached the train station after 10 minutes of a quick walk. While waiting for the train on the platform, he saw far away the roof of the Kashubian prison. He suddenly felt the pain in his heart pass all over his body again and again. He wanted to leave this city as soon as possible and never come back. But as long as Piotr was in the prison, Kamil couldn't possibly leave him behind

When the train arrived, he jumped in quickly and sat down by the window. As the train lumbered out of the city and Kamil saw through the dirty window numerous garden plots, meadows and forests, he felt a slight relief. The car was almost empty and only four individual people were sitting on plastic, shoddy seats lined with cheap red fake leather. The dirty second-class car smelled of body odor and urine from a nearby toilet where the broken door did not close. All the way he tried to read a newspaper that someone had left on the sea. He couldn't concentrate and after a while he couldn't remember what he was reading. After 30 minutes, his journey finally came to the end.

Walking through the town, he smelled the familiar scents of flowers from the home gardens. They reminded him for a moment of the carefree childhood he'd spent here. Oddly enough, this time the whole atmosphere of a small village didn't irritate him at all, like the last time he was here. As he walked past a local store, he waved a hand at several drunks drinking beer outside. Some of them were his father's old friends.

Entering the apartment, he kissed his mother on the cheek.

"Oh you're here quickly." His mother greeted him. "Take off your shoes and come in," she said warmly.

The thick whiskey brown sweater and dark green wool skirt made her look the same as the last time he had seen her. If it wasn't for a few new wrinkles on her face, he could have sworn she wasn't getting old at all. The apartment smelled of the dinner she had prepared in the kitchen.

"Where's Mika?" he asked with anxiety on his face when he was not greeted by his little mongrel as always.

"I don't know what's wrong with her." His mother became said. "She's been on the couch since yesterday and she's not eating anything. I had a hard time taking her outside today to defecate. I think she ate something from the dumpster when she was on a walk yesterday and she got poisoned. I've already given her medical charcoal, but if she doesn't recover by tomorrow, I'll take her to the vet."

Mika was lying on the burgundy sofa on her favorite blue blanket. Seeing Kamil, she waggled her tail tip slightly and got up. Kamil hugged her tenderly, stroked her, and kissed her head lightly. She looked at him with swollen, sick eyes that expressed pain familiar to him. For a moment it seemed to him that by looking at him she wanted to tell him, "I know what has happened and that's why I'm so worried about both of you."

He hugged her again and sat down next to her on the couch. Mika snuggled into his body as if she had found solace.

"Who would have thought that you would like to spend your free days with your mother," she said in surprise, leaning on the chair. "Kamil, has something happened? You look bad," she asked. At this moment she looked at least five years older.

"I just wanted to see how you are doing." He pretended to be confident, but his voice was dispassionate. His face was as dark as if he were about to cry.

"Well, it's all the same with me. My left knee started to hurt a little again. It's probably because of the weather," she said sitting down on the couch next to Kamil and gently massaging her knee.

"Yes, it's definitely down to the weather." He repeated like a wind-up doll, trying to keep up appearances of normality. His body, all hunched, his face terribly white as a sheet of paper, all screaming and calling for help.

"Kamil, are you sure everything is all right? The last time we talked, you were completely different, full of life."

135

"Yes, I think you're right," he said sadly, lowering his head. "Now all my life and energy have escaped from me. I feel like a big balloon, from which somebody has let all the air out," He replied almost sobbing. At the same time, Mika raised her head and tenderly licked his left hand.

"Will you finally tell me what has happened?" His mother raised her voice. As usual in such situations she was showing awkwardly that she was nervous and impatient. But now he saw in her face that she was really worried about him.

"Well," he sighed deeply.

For a moment, his eyes stopped on their family photography from the early 70s standing on a shelf. It was a memorable vacation in Sopot. In the picture, all three of them, including his father, stood by the sea, smiling and full of hope for the future. He would like to turn back and stop the time at that moment.

"Well," he repeated. "One of my good friends was arrested yesterday."

"Oh, my God!" she shouted, all shaken. "I already thought that something must have happened to you. But what about him? Did he have a car crash? Did he steal something? Did he beat his wife?" She grabbed her chin with her right hand.

Her bony white/yellow, almost transparent hand with a line of blue veins, resembled a dried autumn maple leaf from which all life had escaped.

"Mum, none of these things. How to say, he has been considered an enemy of the system, but he is innocent. Nothing was found with him and they have nothing against him."

"Guilty or innocent, this will be decided by the

court. People are not arrested for nothing in this country," she said naively, as if she believed it herself.

"Oh Mum, you don't understand anything," Kamil bridled, looking at her with such reproach as if she was guilty of Piotr's arrest. At that moment something was hissing in the kitchen.

"O, Jesus!" His mother jumped up to the kitchen. "I put the soup on and completely forgot."

After a while two plates of hot tomato soup were already on the coffee table.

"Eat, you will feel better. You look weak."

Because of the smell of fresh tomato soup, despite the lack of hunger, Kamil slowly began to eat.

"Is this Piotr about whom you have told me so much lately?" asked his mother, putting a hand on his shoulder.

Kamil froze for a moment, and almost choked on the soup. He clearly underestimated his mother's instincts.

"Yes, it's him, he replied dryly and concisely, swallowing hard.

Kamil pushed back the plate of unfinished soup. There was awkward silence for a moment.

"You know, son, if he's innocent, they'll definitely release him. It was probably a mistake and everything will be explained shortly."

"Mum, you don't know what you're saying!" said Kamil, sitting back on the couch and looking at his mother like a crazy woman who does not realize the seriousness of the situation.

"Hmm." she suspended her voice for a moment. She sat on the couch and moved closer to her son.

"You must really like him very much. Do you want to tell me something else?" she didn't give in,

137

grabbing Kamil's hand. At first Kamil pulled his hand away from her grip, but after a while their hands were again intertwined.

"You know." he started shyly. "I've never had such a close friend."

"I know, Kamil, maybe if you grew up with an older brother..." she thought for a moment.

"I blame myself all the time for you being an only child. You know, when I gave birth to you, I was very sick for a long time. Women's problems. After that, the doctor told me I couldn't have more children." she said in a low voice.

Kamil had a very embarrassed expression on his face.

"Oh, Mum, I don't blame you. I had a really happy childhood," he said, squeezing his mother's hand tighter.

"I tried my son. I know you always wanted to have an older brother..." She suspended her voice for a moment. She propped her forehead with her hand and while lowering her head, she wiped away her tears surreptitiously. Kamil hugged his mother and Mika snuggled to Kamil again.

They sat there saying nothing for a moment. The time stood still. They were only mother, son and dog hugging each other. They looked like one lump that was being digested from the inside by a disease unknown to anyone.

"I want you to know... mother," he began shyly.

"If your friend's arrest has something to do with you, remember that no matter what happens I will always love you just the way you are. I am your mother who carried you under her heart for nine months. We are like she-wolves who are willing to fight for their young, to the last drop of blood. When the young leave the common nest and they are far away from us, we always sense the danger coming for them beforehand. We mothers, unlike fathers, love our children, not for something but for everything."

Kamil was crying all over, wiping his tears awkwardly with his hand. His mother put her hand on his shoulder.

"It's good that you have someone, because you know, life without love is like traveling one way on a river full of tears. Take care, son."

Kamil, crying, whispered to his mother. "Thank you, Mum, thank you for everything. I love you."

"I love you too, Kamil."

He realized that he had never spoken with his mother so honestly. Their common endearments reminded him of the times of safety and their joined closeness, the days when his mother was his closest friend.

It was almost dark outside. The rain hitting the window ledge gave the impression of heaven's tears weeping over all the injustice of this world.

"I think you should eat something." said his mother, getting up from the couch.

Kamil looked into Mika's eyes, who wagged her tail. Sinking his hand into her fluffy coat, he felt some magical, healing energy flow into his body. Dogs seemed to always have that effect on people.

"Sit at the table," his mother asked. "I got delicious meatballs from Aunt Jadzka."

After this wave of emotion reminiscent of a sudden flood, he felt really hungry.

"Eat and go to sleep," said his mother.

"You know, sometimes in the light of the day, the reality looks completely different," she added, trying to raise his spirits.

He devoured the meatballs and, once finished eating, went to his room.

"Goodnight, Mum."

27th APRIL 1986

The train was slowly reaching the Szczecin Główny station. The last four days that Kamil spent with his mother had allowed him to rest and regenerate.

He returned full of strength, new ideas and with a plan to act. He realized that he should not sit around and worry while Piotr was in custody. What will be in 20 or 30 years? Will he still be hiding and be ashamed to say whom he loves.

He had to start acting in order to damage at least a bit those small cogs of the system that he now hated with a passion.

He got off the train with a brown leather briefcase hanging on his left shoulder and two heavy plastic bags loaded with food prepared by his mother. In his briefcase he had all the leaflets previously hidden on his mother's plot, which Piotr had given him with the machine before his detention.

On the train and at the station, he tried to mix with the crowd to draw as little attention as possible. He was trying to walk home not very quickly so as not to arouse any suspicion.

When he finally got home, he closed the door and put on all the locks. He took out the leaflets from his briefcase and scattered them all over the bed. For some time he was gloating at the sight of them and sniffing the smell of cheap printing ink. In this way, he seemed to be closer to Piotr for a while.

All the leaflets on the bed looked like money from a bank robbery in a distant country unknown to anyone. He imagined that each of them was a pass to the free world. He wanted to go out and start handing out leaflets to random passers-by so as to save as many people as possible in his city.

It was already after 7:00 p.m. He took a beer from the fridge. He began to drink it while devouring homemade garlic sausage that he had brought from his mother. When he finished the beer, he took courage. He decided to go to the prison on Kashubska Street where Piotr stayed, to see what would happen at 8:00 p.m. when the guards changed.

Just in case, he put on old black corduroy trousers, a navy blue hoodie, and a gray baseball cap backwards. Looking at himself in the mirror, he was sure he looked more like a teenager going out for a beer with his friends than a serious civil servant.

It was almost dark when he reached the prison walls. Only one man stood by the wall. He was short, about 50, and had facial hair of several days. He was dressed in gray overalls and a hat made of the same material. He looked like a boiler room worker and certainly worked as a stoker.

It was 8:00 p.m. The man came closer to the wall. After a moment he raised his right hand and waved it in the air. A heavy, hoarse voice said from the cell window on the third floor. "Go ahead!"

The man in the overalls blew out his cheeks as if he was to play the trumpet. Suddenly he shouted in one breath, "To the Gypsy: The young have sorted everything!"

After a few seconds of silence someone from the cell window confirmed. "Gone!

The man in the overalls with evident satisfaction on his face turned around and walked away. It all looked as natural as if he had been coming here everyday for a long time always for the same purpose.

Kamil, emboldened by the whole situation, came over and stood in the same place. Before he could open his mouth, someone from the cell window shouted, Next!

Kamil, without thinking long, exclaimed only, "To the Crow!: The Gray Swan is keeping everything under control!"

After a moment of silence, from the window of the cell he heard the well-known call to him, "Gone!"

After all, he looked around him. When he was certain that he was alone on the street and no one was watching him, he breathed a sigh of relief. Everything had gone easier than he expected.

The evening was warm. Going home, he could only hear the singing of nightingales in the chestnut alley he was returning along. He considered it the launch of his small private plan to disintegrate the system...

30TH APRIL 1986

WUSW Headquarters, Małopolska Street in Szczecin.

The boss was sitting at the desk, in the same slightly crumpled gray jacket that he always wore. He was browsing a daily while picking his teeth and puffing on a cigarette. He was just shaking ash from the cigarette when someone knocked on the door.

"Come in."

"I'm here to report, Sir, that the priest has been arrested," Lieutenant Głogowski informed him

"Were there problems?"

"Not really, but when we searched through the vicarage we found nothing."

"Shit, not good," he sighed, upset.

"Well, almost nothing. We found two letters from his lover. It took us a while, but we checked all the dates and locations, and everything is in order. It's Kamil Adamski from Division B."

The old man's face turned purply red.

"Fucking hell, the what?"

He got so angry that he kicked a cabinet placed next to the desk so hard that the ashtray jumped up.

"So, we train him here and send him to actions, and this sausage fucks a priest?! For fuck's sake, who checked him?" the boss shouted.

"Robert Piotrowski from his Division."

"And? Nothing came up?" he screamed, pissed off.

"No. The last report that came in was from one and a half months ago: '*Situation is stable. The employee is still getting used to the work in our cell. He shows a lot of will and interest in his job.*'"

"Oh fuck!" The old guy sat on a chair, heavily breathing, with his face covered in sweat.

"Bring this Piotrkowski in! Hold the Crow for a few more days, then let him go and observe."

"And what about Adamski, Sir? Plan A or B?"

"What's A!? What's B?" the boss screamed, spitting everywhere. "This is too big of a risk, and he knows too much about us already. Fuck knows what he's already told them. We are going onto Plan C straight away"

1ST MAY 1986

The day was warm, yet cloudy. Kamil was wearing black trousers, a light green T-shirt and a navy, polyamide jacket with numerous pockets. Looking at himself in the mirror, yet again, he made sure he didn't look suspicious in it.

He got to the Grunwaldzki Square at 8:40. The march was to begin at nine and last around three hours. Most people did not like this holiday. May the first was a day off work and a great celebration of the working class. Everyone from various companies, institutions or schools had to take part in the May Day parade, which was to commemorate important events for the workers' community, but unfortunately, it was always purely propaganda. Kamil had liked that day as a child because he didn't have to go to school. Later, when he started working, he realized that this was one very carefully planned show, to which people came more from coercion than for pleasure. As soon as he met Robert and the rest of his colleagues from his department, he felt calmer. Robert was holding a curled-up banner made out of fabric, attached to two sticks.

"Ah, hi, you're here. We were worried we wouldn't be able to pull this off alone," Robert laughed. "You, me and Mariusz are supposed to hold the banner."

"Let me see, what is it?" Kamil asked.

After unrolling the red fabric, a few words appeared in front of Kamil's eyes. It said: '*Every day we write the future of Poland, as well as our own.*'

"We are supposed to be the third in line, right behind the marine school," Robert added.

Kamil looked around. The square was full of people from various work places, schools and universities. Shipyard workers were wearing their uniforms. Hospital staff had white coats, and students—uniforms. In addition, each group held picket signs with slogans corresponding to the nature of their work.

A huge number of different banners could be seen around: '*We are building Poland strong, economically lawful and just*' and so on. Cuban oranges were being sold from a lorry STAR next to the fountain and the queue was now over 50 meters long.

"Oh, look at our boss," Robert nudged him. Kamil looked towards them. The boss seemed to be very happy and you could deduce that he has not only known them for a long time, but also on a personal level. Two fat, tall, gray men, well over 50, in brown suits and snowy white shirts with red ties, talked to the boss. Their impeccably tailored suits indicated that they were the biggest party top dogs. They were patting the boss friendly on the back. The boss was telling something vividly, gesturing with his hands, after which all three laughed. From a distance, everyone looked like three burly, bulky bulldogs from the same kennel. Happy that they always have a full bowl of food and that they are in their own area where they are safe and that they know well.

"He's talking to the biggest top dogs from City Hall. The one on the right is some big cheese from Warsaw."

At exactly 9:05, the march set off from the Grunwaldzki Square towards Wyzwolenia Alley. The first line of marchers were the nurses and doctors from the Clinical Hospital at Pomorzany. Two of them were holding a banner: '*Freedom, Work, Dignity.*' The white aprons they were wearing contrasted with the red balloons they were holding, resembling the Polish flag. Behind them, there were students from the Marine University dressed in marine uniforms and hats. Three of them carried a banner: '*For Poland to grow in strength!*'

Finally, a group of over 300 people set off with a tag '*Citizen's Militia'(*pl. Milicja Obywatelska). Everybody from Kamil's resort joined in at the back. The procession walked slowly. They passed by an old, tall building at Mariana Buczka Street, which Kamil had a look at before. He waited for another five minutes and asked Mariusz to take the banner from him.

"I need the toilet, I saw a restaurant back there," he said firmly.

"Sure, go, said Mariusz taking the banner from Kamil.

Kamil returned to the old building in a few quick steps and went inside unnoticed. His heart was pounding so hard due to all the excitement and fear that it almost jumped out of his chest. He ran up to the fourth floor as fast as he could, tripping over twice on his way. Grabbing it through the material of his jacket, he opened a window he had previously loosened a day earlier and took out at around 700 leaflets with the slogan: '*Release political prisoners!!!*' With two swift moves of his hand, he quickly tossed them out towards the crowd walking below.

There was no way back from this anymore. He felt that he did the right thing, and that Piotr would have been proud of him. After all this, he closed the window and ran downstairs. He left the building onto the backyard and ran into the building next door, which he used to get out onto the street.

Heading for the front of the march, he saw a crowd collecting the leaflets and the police shouting something through megaphones.

"Shit, I barely found you," he said, running up to his friends, gasping for air.

"We thought you got lost," Mariusz laughed.

" Sorry, I have diarrhea," he said in a quiet voice, leaning towards Robert and Mariusz with a slight grimace.

"Sure, no problems," Robert assured him.

* * *

The sun was gradually piercing through the clouds and it was getting warmer. Imperceptibly, he took his jacket off and tied it around his waist. He slowly looked around checking to see if anybody had realized his absence; he quickly relaxed. Looking around at people, he felt as if they were all a part of some badly directed performance, which they were forced to attend. A list of people who attended the march was made every year by their unit. An absence would have to be thoroughly explained in the boss' office and would mean various problems with taking holidays off, promotions and so on.

During the march, Kamil swapped carrying the

banner with Mariusz and Robert two more times. They stopped a few times on their way, waving and greeting people who were looking out their widows, as well as the ORMO's who stood around the pavements.

Gradually, the march was coming to an end as they were slowly approaching the Grunwaldzki Square. When they stepped onto Malczewskiego Street, this time, Kamil asked Robert to carry the banner.

"Fuck, my stomach, I'll be right back. There's a café nearby," he said to the boys.

As soon as he distanced himself from his group, he walked into the gate to the building on Malczewskiego Street and ran to the top floor. He was drenched though due to fear, stress and the high temperature, and the sweat flowed down his head in streams. He struggled to open the window for a moment because it was jammed. He held his breath, his heart pounding like crazy. He almost gave up and wanted to run downstairs, but after a minute he heard somebody walking all the way down the stairs. He breathed out, pulled the handle once more and the window loosened. He took out all the remaining leaflets that he had in his pockets, sorted them into two piles and pushed them off the windowsill. He closed the window and vigorously ran down the stairs. Just like last time, he jumped out onto the backyard connected to the next building and left for the street unrecognized by anyone. When he got to the square, the march was already over. Robert was talking to their boss, his face twisted in an angry scowl about something.

"Oi, I'm here now, I'm in deep shit today," Kamil joked in a very firm voice.

"Have you heard? Someone threw leaflets around," said Mariusz.

"No way. Where?!" he was surprised and slightly scared. "What happened?" he asked Robert, who had just come up to them.

"Yeah, the boss is well pissed off. The 'Solidarities' have scattered some leaflets around the streets during the march, but our people have already taken care of this."

"How many were there?" Kamil asked stupidly.

"We're not sure exactly. Around 1,000, maybe 1,500. We were able to pick up some, but not the majority of them," said Robert disappointed.

"There's nothing we can do, there will always be some units in the society," Mariusz pulled a sour face. "A pint, then, gentlemen?" he offered.

"Sure!" said Kamil happily.

"It's on me today!"

"Well, I don't think we'll argue with that, "Robert and Mariusz laughed.

They walked slowly towards the nearest restaurant. Kamil realized he had never been this proud of himself and he couldn't wait to tell Piotr all about it.

6TH MAY 1986

Teatr Współczesny in Szczecin, director Paprocki's office.

Paprocki was sipping his tea looking through the *Film* magazine when somebody knocked on the door.

"Good morning, may I come in for a minute, Director?"

"Oh, it's you, Mr. Milewski, please come in and have a seat," said the director putting his newspaper aside.

"What's the story of this incident during the Sunday's performance?" asked Paprocki. "Well, haven't you heard?" started Milewski glad that he could enlighten the director. "Apparently Fabisiak is a squealer and they arrested some priest because of him. It's probably deeper than that, as people say that priest supposedly had ties with the Resistance. Somebody wrote the word 'SNITCH' in red paint on the advertising poster of Fabisiak outside. A different poster in the city centre says, 'GRASS UP!'.

'Who would have thought that Fabisiak was an informer?" asked the director, raising his eyebrows high. At the same time, he twisted his face in discontent and scratched his cheek, looking very surprised.

Milewski, clearly in his element, went on. "What's more," Milewski continued excited, "during the Sunday performance, someone from the audience threw a rotten egg at Fabisiak. It was probably a churchgoer from that priest's parish. It's a good thing he'd missed, otherwise we would have had to end the play. Additionally, at the end of the spectacle, a few people began to whistle. The cashier also told me that over 100 tickets were returned."

Seeing the director's face get red from rage and fury, Milewski felt a sense of accomplishment. He had gotten what he came there for. He wanted to throw dirt on Fabisiak, and he succeeded.

"I'll be damned," screamed the director whose eyes nearly popped out of their sockets. "Shit! That's all we needed now, a scandal! We are putting *Poszukiwany, poszukiwana* on hold until the whole thing calms down," he decided harshly. "We are changing the repertoire! We are going back to *Śluby panieńskie* and *Zemsta* from Monday on, and Fabisiak is going on administrative leave…'

8TH MAY 1986
Prison, Kaszubska Street in Szczecin

Cell 5A with a little window through which light could barely shine, on the second floor, was three by three meters, had yellow, spoiled walls and a bunk bed. There were a few pictures of naked women on the walls and a lot of writing all over them, two pieces of which stood out from the rest. *"Suffering requires more effort than death"* and the second, which Piotr would look at every morning when he woke up *"Only God can judge me"*. Additionally, there was a sink and a toilet recess. There was a small, wooden table with an oilcloth and two navy, worn-down stools in the middle of the cell. Apart from Piotr, there were three more convicts in the cell: two thieves and a rapist.

"Graczyk Piotr."

"That's me," Piotr jumped up.

"Date of birth?"

"Seventh of August 1955."

"Parent's names?"

"Stanisław, Jadwiga."

"With me."

Piotr walked across the whole second floor following the guard. They passed around 20 cells and walked down the stairs to the ground floor to the main call room.

"You're free to go, Graczyk. Here are your things. Sign this."

Piotr was surprised with this whole situation unsure whether it was just a part of some larger game. When he stepped outside, he still couldn't believe he was released.

How do I get in touch with Kamil? They're probably watching me. Is our machine still at his mother's? These questions, with no answers, were stuck in his head. Most of all, however, he wanted to see Kamil, especially since he was quite close to his district. However, he knew that this could be too dangerous for the both of them.

* * *

It was almost 10:00 in the evening. Kamil was slowly getting ready for bed. He kept on thinking about Piotr and whether the message he had screamed on the street had really reached him. It was two weeks since Piotr was arrested and Kamil still had no word from him. The impotence and powerlessness that there was nothing he could do to change Piotr's situation was the worst. When he began to read the newspaper, someone called his door. He was a bit surprised, because he wasn't expecting anyone at this time. When he peeked through the door, he saw Ms. Maria, the lady from the vicarage. He quickly opened the door. She was wearing a babushka and looked just like he remembered her. The woman was holding a letter. Passing it to Kamil, she said quietly, "They let him go."

Then she turned around and walked down the stairs. Kamil barely had time to scream, "Thank you!"

Dear Kamil,

I was released today at 3 P.M. I hope you're well and healthy, and that you managed to skillfully get rid of the things I gave you. When they let me out, I wanted to come to you straight away, but I realize they're watching me. Meet me tomorrow, at 6 p.m. at Dziewoklicz . I'll be on the bridge, fishing. Be careful!!!

Love you,
Your Grey Swan.

Kamil read the letter two more times in disbelief.

They let him out! God, I'm so happy! I need to get rid of that machine from my mum's shed as quickly as possible. I'll visit her the day after tomorrow and it will be best if I throw the suitcase into Oder he thought.

* * *

He tossed and turned in his bed. His mind was racing. *Did Piotr lose that much weight? How did they treat him there? Was he beaten? Even if he looks miserable, I can't show it. Did he give someone up? Maybe that someone was me?* He found that last thought outright funny. He'd confided in Piotr. Piotr was his personal hero.

Finally, he went to the kitchen and finished the vodka he had left in the fridge. After going to bed a few minutes after that, he felt slightly relaxed. The alcohol was finally beginning to take effect. He fell asleep within 20 minutes, but unfortunately, not for long…

9TH MAY 1986

As always, Kamil got up at quarter to seven. He was all excited to finally see Piotr. He couldn't sleep all night and only managed to fall asleep in the early morning. It looked like the day would be beautiful and sunny. The sun warmed Kamil's room with its delicate rays. He impulsively turned the radio on:

Nie wyobrażam sobie, miły,
Abyś na wojnę kiedyś szedł.
Życia nie wolno tracić, miły,
Życie jest po to, by kochać się

[Eng.
I can't imagine, my dear,
For you to go to war.
You cannot give up life, my dear,
Since life is here to love.]

Kora was singing.

God, what a sad song. They should not play such depressing songs during happy days, like this, he thought.

Despite the sleepless night, some amazing energy was buzzing inside him. He was counting the minutes down to his meeting with Piotr. He was wondering what to say when they met, and whether his arrest had changed anything.

The smell of lilac mixed with the scent of acacia trees flowering along the road. All the flowers and trees were blooming to their fullest outside, and you could smell the coming summer. Walking down the street, Kamil was almost smiling to the people passing by. *Today is going to be a great day, I can feel it!* he thought.

Crossing the street, he spotted a cashier from his bakery smoking a cigarette outside. Suddenly, a large Fiat 125p came from behind the block. A car with no registration plates, racing at a crazy speed, hit Kamil with all its power. His body flew a few meters, falling unconsciously on the ground. A stream of blood flowed from his mouth.

"Jesus! A man was murdered!!!" the horrified bakery cashier began to scream.

"People! Call for an ambulance!" she shouted.

A man passing by on the other side of the road ran up to Kamil's body. People began to run out from the nearest building. A few people gathered around the body. Someone from the crowd asked, "Is he alive?"

"I don't know, I can't feel the pulse…"

Epilogue

Operation Hyacinth itself was not connected with my life in any way. All this happened in 1985 and I was only 13 years old at the time.

The only escape from our gray everyday life was Western music that was not forbidden and was often played on the radio. Foreign hits mainly from the UK or the US gave us hope for a better future and the belief that somewhere far away people live normally without fighting every day for their survival.

I was just discovering my sexuality as a gay teenager. Madonna was a very special person to me, as an idol. She was fighting for tolerance and was already supporting people with HIV. By breaking the rules, she showed me that I was not alone in the world and that I should accept myself as a gay man. She has been my icon, and I don't know if I would be who I am today if it were not for Madonna.

In Poland, the iron curtain collapsed in 1989. We had an independent government elected in free elections. The beginning of the 1990s in Poland ushered in huge social and economic changes. The free market allowed people to set up their own businesses. Ordinary citizens slowly began to get rich and explore the world getting to know other cultures and people.

The first official gay clubs and pubs began to appear in larger cities.

In 1990, the first official gay magazine *Inaczej* (Otherwise), was published. Even today I remember the day when I bought the first issue. I was 17 at the time and although I grew up in a city of 400,000 inhabitants, I didn't know any other gay men. I read every page with high color on my face. It was there where I read the article about Operation Hyacinth for the first time. I was shocked that something like this happened not so long ago. I thought about it all night and couldn't sleep. I realized that if I had been born a few years earlier, I would have been persecuted just like the people in the article. When I woke up the next morning, I thought there must have been a lot of different stories going on during this action. After several minutes, the whole story of Kamil, an SB employee and Piotr, who is a priest, was ready in my head from the first to the last chapter. Because everything was happening in very difficult times, the story must have had such an ending.

I wanted the novel to take place on two levels. Kamil and Piotr are full of ideals, young and struggling with the system. They wanted to live a real life and not for real and thus paid the highest price. In comparison with them, Fabisiak, who was broken, intimidated and surrendered by the system. For the younger generation and people who grew up in normal, free, democratic countries, it will be easier to understand how the whole system of human surveillance worked, how individuals were intimidated, broken and enslaved by various methods.

I didn't mean any specific people I knew when writing this story. Of course, Kamil mostly has my characteristics. Piotr is rather the figure of the perfect lover whom each of us once met or is still looking for. Each of us could be Fabisiak. I find some of his character traits in myself.

Currently, for most of us, the only worry is a too high loan payment or bad weather during vacations. Despite the lofty slogans and ideals that we think we are able to fight for in our lives, none of us really knows how we would behave if we had to live in those times and had to make choices that would not always depend on our own life but sometimes on the whole groups of people.

I think *Operation Hyacinth* can be a unique history lesson, especially for the younger generation who don't always appreciate what they have at their disposal today, generations that are growing up in the age of the Internet and of all current prosperity. By showing the story of Kamil and Piotr, I wanted to show the younger generation what difficult times people had to live in under a totalitarian system.

Of course, there is still a lot to do in Poland. The situation of LGBT people, due to the hostile or indifferent attitude of the Polish government, has not changed much in the last 20 years. The situation is difficult because of the high position of the Catholic Church in Poland, which has a great influence on the ruling groups.

Despite the sad ending, I think that *Operation Hyacinth* can bring hope and a positive message for the future. It is thanks to Kamil and Piotr, their dedication, fight for love and their ideals that the younger generations are now growing up mostly in free, tolerant countries. They are not afraid to say

Pawel Kurczab

aloud who they are. They can speak if their human rights are violated. They associate in organizations, organize parades, have their own clubs and pubs, get married and adopt children. They live today in a world, which for the generation of Kamil and Piotr was only a utopia and an unfulfilled dream.

About the Author

Pawel Kurczab was born on the 5th of December 1972 in Limanowa (Poland). He holds a BS in Sociology from the University of Szczecin. Over the years, he has worked as a paramedic, a social worker and a probation officer.

Pawel has always been a student of social psychology and the sociology of culture. As a sociologist, he wanted to present the Hyacinth action from an individual's experience and not in the form of a documentary or reportage, as it has been the case so far. Since 2007, he has been living in England (the UK) where he works for the National Health Service.

Operation *Hyacinth* is his first novel. He has now started working on his second novel.

If You Enjoyed This Book, Please Consider These Other Riverdale Avenue Books Titles

The Passionate Attention of an Interesting Man
By Ethan Mordden

The Red Shoes
By John Stewart Wynne

50 Shades of Gay
By Jeffery Self

Monarch Season
By Mario Lopez-Cordero

Playing by the Book
By Chris Shirley